# MAIGRET AND THE WINE MERCHANT

TRANSLATED FROM THE FRENCH
BY EILEEN ELLENBOGEN

## GEORGES SIMENON

Tess Press

Design by edstudio

ISBN: 1-57912-579-4

Manufactured in the United States

jihgfedcba

# MAIGRET AND
# THE WINE MERCHANT

# CHAPTER 1

"You killed her in order to steal from her, didn't you?"

"I never meant to kill her. It was only a toy pistol I had. That proves it, surely?"

"Did you know she had a lot of money?"

"I didn't know how much. She'd worked hard all her life, and she was eighty-two or -three. I knew she must have a bit put by."

"How often did you ask her for money?"

"I don't know. Several times. She knew that was why I went to see her. She was my grandmother. She always handed me five francs. I ask you! What use is five francs to a man out of work?"

Maigret felt weighed down, discouraged, a little sad. This was a commonplace thing, a sordid crime such as happened almost every week, a lonely old woman robbed and murdered by a boy who was not yet twenty. The only difference was that, in this case, Théo Stiernet had killed his own grandmother.

He was taking it all very calmly, really astonishingly so, in fact, and seemed only too willing to co-operate. He was plump and flabby, with a round face and almost no chin. He had

protuberant eyes, and thick lips, so red that at first glance
Maigret thought he had been using lipstick.

"Five francs! Just like doling out pocket money to a kid!"

"Was she a widow?"

"Her husband died nearly forty years ago. She had a little
dry goods shop on the Place Saint-Paul for a long time, but a
couple of years ago, when she began finding it hard to get about,
she gave it up."

"Have you got a father?"

"He's in a nut-house—Bicêtre."

"Is your mother still alive?"

"I don't live with her, haven't for years. She's never sober."

"Any brothers and sisters?"

"One sister. She left home when she was fifteen, and she
hasn't been heard of since."

His tone was quite matter-of-fact.

"How did you know your grandmother kept her money in
the house?"

"She didn't believe in banks, or the Post Office either."

It was nine o'clock at night, just twenty-four hours since
the murder had been committed, in an old house on the Rue
du Roi-de-Sicile, in which Joséphine Ménard occupied two
rooms on the third floor. One of the fourth-floor tenants had
met Stiernet on the stairs, on his way out. She knew him well
by sight. They had exchanged greetings.

At about half past nine, Madame Palloc, whose rooms, on
the third floor, were opposite those of Madame Ménard, went
to call on the old lady, as she often did.

She knocked, but got no answer. She tried the door and,
finding it open, went in. Joséphine Ménard was lying dead in
a heap on the floor, her skull cracked open, her face battered
to a pulp.

It had not taken them long to track down Théo Stiernet. He was found, at six o'clock the next morning, fast asleep on a bench at the Gare du Nord.

"What did you have to kill her for?"

"I never meant to. She went for me, and I panicked."

"You threatened her with your toy pistol, I suppose?"

"Yes. She didn't turn a hair. Maybe she could see it was just a toy.

"'Get out!' she said. 'It takes more than a bum like you to scare me!'

"There was a pair of scissors lying on that round table of hers. She grabbed them, and came at me with them.

"'Get out! Get out!' she kept repeating, 'Or you'll regret it for the rest of your life.'

"She was tiny, very frail-looking, but she had a wicked temper.

"She scared the wits out of me, coming at me like that with the open scissors. She could have blinded me. I looked around for something to defend myself with, and grabbed the first thing I saw, the poker. It was lying beside the stove."

"How many times did you strike her?"

"I don't know. She wouldn't go down. She just went on standing there, staring at me."

"Was there blood on her face?"

"Yes. I didn't want to hurt her. I don't know. I just went on hitting her."

Maigret could almost hear the Public Prosecutor addressing the Court of Assize:

"Thus, the accused Stiernet, with bestial ferocity, struck down his ill-fated victim."

"When you saw her crumpled on the floor, what then?"

"I just stared at her. I didn't understand. I hadn't meant to kill her. That's how it was, I swear. You must believe me."

"All the same, it didn't stop you from going through her drawers."

"That was later. My first thought was to get away. But before I got to the door, I remembered that all the money I had in the world was a franc and a fifty-centime piece. I'd just been turned out of my room because I owed them three weeks' rent."

"So you turned back?"

"Yes. The way you put it, you'd think I'd turned the apartment inside out. That's not true. I just looked into one or two drawers. In one of them I found an old purse and slipped it into my pocket. Then I came across a couple of rings and a cameo brooch in a cardboard box."

The two rings, the cameo brooch, and the shabby purse were lying on Maigret's desk, next to his pipe rack.

"So you didn't find her savings?"

"I didn't look. I couldn't get away fast enough. I couldn't stand the sight of her, lying there. Her eyes seemed to follow me all around the room. On the stairs, on my way out, I ran into Madame Menou. I went into a bar and ordered a brandy. Then, since there were sandwiches on the bar, I ate three."

"Were you hungry?"

"I must have been, I suppose. I ate my sandwiches, had a cup of coffee, and then began wandering around the streets. After all that, I was no better off, really, because it turned out that there were only eight francs, twenty-five in the purse.

*"So after all, I was no better off, really!"*

He had said this as though it were the most natural thing in the world. Maigret, fascinated and horrified, stared at him.

"What made you choose the Gare du Nord?"

"I didn't. I just happened to find myself there. It was very cold."

It was the fifteenth of December. There was a north wind blowing, creating little eddies among the snowflakes before they settled, like a film of dust, on the sidewalks.

"Were you thinking of crossing the frontier into Belgium?"

"How could I, with barely five or six francs to my name?"

"What were your plans?"

"First of all, to get some sleep."

"Did you expect to be arrested?"

"I hadn't thought."

"What were you thinking about?"

"Nothing."

He had not found the money, but the police had. It was on top of the mirror-fronted wardrobe, wrapped in brown paper, all twenty-two thousand francs of it.

"What would you have done if you had found the money?"

"I don't know."

The door of Maigret's office opened, and Lapointe came in.

"I've just had Inspector Fourquet on the phone. He wanted to speak to you, but I told him you were busy."

Fourquet was attached to the XVIIth Arrondissement, a wealthy upper-middle-class residential district, where murder was almost unheard of.

"There's been a murder on the Rue Fortuny, a couple of hundred yards from the Parc Monceau. If the papers found on him are anything to go by, the victim is a man of some standing, a big wholesale wine merchant."

"Anything else known?"

"Apparently he was walking to his car when he was shot. Four shots were fired. There were no witnesses. The street is a dead end, and it was deserted at the time."

Catching sight of Stiernet, Maigret gave a little shrug.

"Is Lucas in?"

He went over to the door. Lucas was at his desk.

"Can you spare a minute?"

Stiernet glanced casually from one to the other, his bulging eyes expressing little interest or concern.

"I want you to take over for me. You'd better start again from scratch, and when you've got a signed statement from him, take him down to the cells. I want you to come with me, Lapointe."

He put on his heavy black overcoat and wound a navy-blue woolen scarf around his neck. Madame Maigret had just finished knitting it for him. He stopped in the doorway to take a last look at the prisoner, then refilled his pipe, lit it, and went off down the corridor.

The night was still young, but there were very few people about, and their faces looked pinched with cold. Even the thickest winter clothing could not keep out the biting north wind. The two men got into one of the little black police cars parked in the forecourt, and drove almost to the other side of Paris in record time.

There were a couple of police officers at the approaches to the Rue Fortuny, diverting traffic and moving on bystanders who had come to stare at the body lying on the sidewalk. Four or five men were bustling about near the body, Fourquet among them.

He came forward to meet Maigret.

"The Divisional Superintendent has just arrived, with the doctor."

Maigret shook hands with the superintendent, whom he knew well. He was a man of friendly disposition, and he wore his clothes with style.

"Did you know Oscar Chabut?"

"Should I have known him?"

"He was a man of some standing, a wholesale wine merchant—Le Vin des Moines, one of the biggest firms in Paris. You must have seen the name on walls and delivery trucks. There's a whole fleet of barges and tankers, too."

The man lying on the sidewalk was heavily built, though not fat. He had the physique of a football player. The doctor stood up and dusted the powdery snow from the knees of his trousers.

"He must have died within two or three minutes at most. We'll know more after the autopsy."

Maigret looked into the staring eyes. They were very light blue, almost a watery gray. The features were strongly formed, especially the powerful jaw, which was already beginning to sag.

The van from Criminal Records drew up at the curb, and the technicians got out and began unloading their equipment, for all the world like a movie or television camera crew on location.

"Have you been in touch with the Public Prosecutor's Office?"

"Yes. They're sending over a Deputy and an Examining Magistrate."

Maigret looked around for Fourquet. He was standing only a few feet away, flapping his long arms and slapping his thighs, trying to keep warm.

"Which is his car?"

There were five or six parked in the street, all expensive-looking. Chabut's was a red Jaguar.

"Have you looked in the glove compartment?"

"Yes. A pair of sunglasses, a Michelin Guide, two road maps of Provence, and a box of cough drops."

"He must have been coming out of one of the houses in this street."

It was not a long block. Maigret, turning around to look at the houses, recognized the one in front of which the body still lay on the sidewalk. It was built in the style popular in 1900, with fancy stonework, carved with arabesques, surrounding the windows. The front door was of brass-studded oak, with a small barred window let into it, and Maigret sensed rather than saw that the panel behind the bars had moved.

"Come with me, Lapointe."

He went up to the door and rang the bell. There was an appreciable pause before the panel slid back, to reveal an eye and the outline of a woman's shoulder. There was no light in the passage behind her.

"Who's there?"

Maigret recognized the voice.

"Good evening, Blanche."

"What do you want?"

"Don't you remember me, Chief Superintendent Maigret? It's true, it must be all of ten years since we last met."

Without waiting to be invited in, he opened the door.

"Come on in," he said to Lapointe. "You're too young, of course, to have known Madame Blanche, as she was always called."

As if familiar with the layout of the house, Maigret switched on the light and made straight for the double doors, which led into a spacious reception room carpeted with overlapping rugs. There were heavy draped curtains over the windows, tapestries on the walls, and multicolored cushions everywhere. The room was softly lit by table lamps with silk shades.

Madame Blanche looked about fifty, though in fact she would never see sixty again. She was small and plump. She was generally considered to be very distinguished-looking. She wore a black silk dress, relieved by several strands of pearls.

"Busy as ever, and still the soul of discretion?"

When Maigret had first known her, thirty years before, she was still on the streets, around the Boulevard de la Madeleine, a very pretty girl with gentle manners and a ready, attractive smile which brought dimples into her cheeks.

Later, she had taken over the management of an apartment on the Rue Notre-Dame-de-Lorette, where a large number of pretty girls were always to be found.

Since then, she had gone up in the world. She was now the owner of this richly appointed mansion, where luxury accommodation with every comfort, including the best whisky and champagne, was available for couples wishing to meet in discreet surroundings.

Whatever she may have thought of Maigret's appearance on the scene, she was putting a good face on it.

"How did it happen?" asked the Chief Superintendent.

"Nothing has happened here. I can't tell you what happened out there, though there's been a lot of coming and going, I've noticed."

"Didn't you hear the shots?"

"Oh, they were shots, were they? I thought it was a car backfiring."

"Where were you, at the time?"

"To tell you the truth, I was having my evening snack in the kitchen, just a roll with a little ham. I never eat dinner."

"Who else was in the house?"

"No one. Why?"

"Who was with Oscar Chabut?"

"Who is Oscar Chabut?"

"You would do well to co-operate, otherwise I'll have to ask you to go with me to the Quai des Orfèvres."

"I don't know the surnames of my clients. They're nearly all people of some standing."

"And you only open the door to them after you've had a look at them through the small window?"

"This is a respectable establishment. I don't let just anybody in, which is no doubt why I am spared the attentions of the Vice Squad."

"Were you watching through the little window when Chabut left?"

"Why should you think that?"

"Lapointe, you'd better take her to the Quai. Maybe she'll have more to say for herself there."

"I can't leave the house. I'll tell you all I know. I take it that, by Chabut, you mean the client who left about half an hour ago?"

"Was he a regular? Did he come often?"

"From time to time."

"What do you mean by that? Once a month? Once a week?"

"More like once a week."

"Always with the same companion?"

"Not always, no."

"What about the one he was with this time? Had you seen her before?"

She hesitated, then said, with a shrug:

"I don't see why I should land myself in trouble for her. She's been here about thirty times in the past year."

"Did he telephone to say he was coming?"

"That's the usual thing."

"What time did they arrive?"

"About seven."

"Separately or together?"

"Together. You couldn't miss that red car of his."

"Did they order anything to drink?"

"I had champagne on ice waiting for them."

"Where's the woman?"

"But . . . She's gone."

"You mean she left after Chabut was shot?"

She looked a little uneasy.

"Of course not!"

"Are you saying that she left before him?"

"It's the truth."

"I'm sorry, Blanche, I don't believe it."

In the course of his work he had often had occasion to visit houses of this sort, and he knew their ways. He was therefore aware of the fact that invariably it was the man who left first, while his companion stayed behind to freshen up and attend to her hair and make-up.

"I want to see the room they used. You stay here, Lapointe, and see that no one leaves the house. Now then, where did you put them?"

"On the first floor. The rose room."

The walls were paneled with wood, and the staircase, with its thick, pale blue carpet held in place by triangular brass clips, had an elaborately carved balustrade.

"When I saw you arrive . . ."

"So you were watching at the little window?"

"What do you think? Naturally, I was anxious to find out what was going on. As soon as I saw you and recognized you, I knew I was in for trouble."

"You did know who he was, didn't you? You might as well admit it."

"Yes."

"What about his companion?"

"Only her Christian name, honest to God. It's Anne-Marie. I always call her the Grasshopper."

"Why is that?"

"Because she's very tall and thin, with unusually long arms and legs."

"Where is she?"

"I told you. She left before him."

"And I told you I don't believe you."

She opened a door to reveal a very plushy bedroom, in which a housemaid was changing the sheets on the canopied bed. On a pedestal table stood a bottle of champagne and two glasses, one of which was not quite empty, and stained with lipstick.

"See for yourself. . . ."

"I see that she's not here or in the bathroom. So far so good. How many other rooms have you?"

"Eight."

"Any of them occupied?"

"No. Mostly, my clients come either in the late afternoon or after dinner. I was expecting one at nine, but he must have seen all those people out there, and . . ."

"Show me the other rooms."

There were four on the first floor, all furnished more or less in the massive style of the Second Empire, with a good deal of drapery in faded colors.

"As you see, there's no one here."

"Keep on going."

"Whatever would she be doing up there?"

"I couldn't say, but I want to see for myself."

The first two rooms on the floor above were, indeed, empty, but in the third there was a girl sitting bolt upright in an over-stuffed chair upholstered in claret-colored velvet.

She sprang to her feet. She was tall and thin, with a flat chest and narrow hips.

"Who is this?" Maigret asked.

"She's waiting for the client I was expecting at nine."

"Do you know her?"

"No."

The girl looked very young, barely twenty. She shrugged, as though to say, What the hell?

"He's bound to find out sooner or later. He's a policeman, isn't he?"

"Chief Superintendent Maigret."

"No kidding!"

She looked at him with interest.

"You don't mean that you're looking into this business yourself?"

"As you see."

"Is he dead?"

"Yes."

She turned to Madame Blanche and said reproachfully:

"Why did you lie to me? You told me he was only wounded."

"How was I to know? I didn't go out to look."

"Who are you, Mademoiselle?"

"My name is Anne-Marie Boutin. I'm his private secretary."

"Did you often come here with him?"

"Usually about once a week. It was always a Wednesday, because that's the evening when I'm supposed to be at my English class."

"Come downstairs," said Maigret, grumpily.

He had had about as much as he could take of pastel colors and soft lighting, in which faces appeared blurred, as though seen through a mist.

They had stopped in the reception room, but it had not occurred to any of them to sit down. They could hear voices, and footsteps coming and going outside, where the icy north wind was still blowing. Indoors, however, the heat was suffocating, as in a hothouse, and, as in a hothouse, there were gigantic tropical plants everywhere, in ornate Chinese pots.

"What do you know about the murder of your employer?"

"Only what she told me," replied the Grasshopper, indicating Madame Blanche. "That someone shot at him and wounded him, and that the concierge next door came running out into the street. She must have telephoned for the police, I suppose, because they were here within minutes."

It was no distance from the police station on the Avenue de Villiers.

"Was he killed outright?"

"Yes."

She did not break down at this, but merely turned a little pale. She appeared more shocked than grieved. She went on, as though scarcely aware of what she was saying:

"I wanted to leave at once, but she wouldn't let me."

Maigret turned to Madame Blanche.

"Why not?"

"Your men were at the door. She would have walked straight into them. I was hoping to keep her out of it. I didn't want to get involved. I knew it would bring the reporters swarming, and that would almost certainly mean the end of this place."

"Tell me exactly what you saw. Where was the man when he fired?"

"Facing the door, in the street, between two parked cars."

"Did you get a good look at him?"

"No. The nearest street lamp is some way off. His face was just a blur."

"Was he tall?"

"No, below average height, I'd say. He was broad-shouldered, though, and wearing dingy clothes. He fired three or four times, I think. I wasn't counting. Monsieur Oscar clutched his stomach, swayed a little, and then fell forward."

Maigret noted that although the girl looked horrified, she did not appear by any means heartbroken.

"Did you love him?"

"I don't know what you mean."

"How long had you been his mistress?"

She looked a little taken aback.

"I don't think you quite understand. When he wanted me, he would say so, but there was never any question of love. I certainly never thought of him as my lover."

"What time are you expected home?"

"Between half past nine and ten. My mother will begin to worry if I'm late."

"Where do you live?"

"Rue Caulaincourt, near the Place Constantin-Pecqueur."

"Where do you work?"

"Quai de Charenton, out beyond the Bercy warehouses."

"Will you be there tomorrow?"

"Certainly."

"It's possible that I'll need your help. Lapointe, see her to the Métro, will you. The papers may already have got wind of this, and I don't want her harassed by reporters."

He was fidgeting with his pipe, feeling that it would perhaps be inappropriate to smoke in these surroundings. All the same, after some hesitation, he did eventually light up.

Madame Blanche stood calmly watching him, her hands folded on her rounded stomach, with an air of irreproachable rectitude.

"Are you quite sure you didn't recognize the man who fired the shots?"

"I swear I didn't."

"Did your client ever come here with a married woman?"

"Very likely, I should think."

"Did he come often?"

"Sometimes two or three times in one week, and then I wouldn't see him for ten or fifteen days. But an interval as long as that was unusual."

"Did anyone ever telephone to make inquiries about him?"

"No."

The Deputy Public Prosecutor and the Examining Magistrate had gone. The temperature outside had dropped still further. The men from the Forensic Laboratory, having lifted the body of the wine merchant onto a stretcher, were lifting it into the mortuary van.

The technicians from Criminal Records were loading their gear into their smaller van.

"Did you find anything?"

"The cartridges. All four of them. 6.35 caliber."

That ruled out a professional gunman. Only an amateur or a woman would use so small a weapon, which could not kill except at very close range.

"No sign of the press?"

"There were a couple of reporters. They went off in rather a hurry. They were anxious to get their stories in in time for the regional editions."

Inspector Fourquet stood patiently by, stamping his feet, and holding a handkerchief up to his face, in an attempt to protect his nose from the biting cold.

"Had he been in there?"

"Yes," said Maigret, grudgingly.

"What will you tell the press?"

"As little as I can get away with. Have you got his wallet and identity papers?"

Fourquet took them from his pocket and handed them over. "What's his home address?"

"Place des Vosges. I forget the number, but it's on his identity card. Are you going to break the news to his wife?"

"It would be kinder, I think, than leaving her to read the whole lurid story in the morning papers."

Maigret could see the entrance to the Malesherbes Métro station at the junction with the Avenue de Villiers, and Lapointe walking away from it with long, brisk strides.

"Thanks for telephoning me, Fourquet. I'm sorry to have kept you hanging about so long out here. You must be frozen."

He got into the snug little police car. Lapointe climbed into the driver's seat and looked inquiringly at the Chief.

"Place des Vosges."

They drove in silence. Fine, powdery snow was still falling, and the gilt-tipped railings of the Parc Monceau were covered with a thin film of frost. They drove along the Champs-Elysées and approached the Place des Vosges by way of the Quais. It did not take them long to get there.

The concierge, invisible in the darkened lodge, pressed a time switch, and lights came on everywhere.

"Madame Chabut," mumbled Maigret, as they went past the lodge.

She did not ask him what his business was. The two men went up to the first floor. On a little brass plate let into the heavy oak door they read the name "Oscar Chabut." It was just half past ten. Maigret rang the bell. After a brief pause the door was opened by a girl in a starched cap and apron. She was a pretty girl, dark, with a good figure. Her uniform, a close-fitting black silk dress, suited her admirably. She looked at them inquiringly.

"Madame Chabut . . ."

"Your name, please?"

"Chief Superintendent Maigret, Criminal Investigation Department."

"Wait here, please."

Amplified voices could be heard declaiming in one of the rooms, a radio or television play, no doubt. Then the voices were cut off in mid-speech, and a second or two later a woman in an emerald green dressing gown appeared, looking puzzled.

She was a beautiful woman, probably in her late thirties. Maigret was particularly struck by her fine carriage and the grace with which she moved.

"Please come in."

She ushered them into a very spacious drawing room. The armchair in which she had been sitting was still drawn up in front of the now blank television screen.

"Please sit down. I hope you haven't come to tell me that my husband has met with an accident."

"I'm afraid we have, Madame."

"Is he hurt?"

"Worse than that."

"You mean . . . ?"

He nodded.

"Poor Oscar!"

The dead man's secretary had shed no tears when told of his death. Neither did his wife. She merely looked downcast and rather sorrowful.

"Was he alone in the car?"

"It wasn't a motor accident. Someone shot him."

"A woman?"

"No. A man."

"Poor Oscar!" she repeated. "Where did it happen?"

And, seeing Maigret's hesitation, she went on:

"You needn't be afraid to tell me. I know what was going on. There hadn't been anything like that between us for years. We were more like good friends than husband and wife. He was quite a dear, really. Only people got the wrong idea because he was always puffing out his chest and banging on the table."

"Do you know the Rue Fortuny?"

"That's where he nearly always took them. I've even met Madame Blanche—a delightful creature! He was eager to show me the place. As I told you, we were very good friends. Whom was he with?"

"A young girl, his private secretary."

"The Grasshopper! That was his name for her, now everyone calls her by it."

Lapointe gaped at her, aghast at her cool self-assurance.

"Was he shot in the house?"

"No. It happened outside on the sidewalk, as your husband was going toward his car."

"Have you arrested the killer?"

"Unfortunately, there was plenty of time before the police arrived for him to get to the Métro, at the head of the street, and jump onto any one of a dozen trains. Since you were so fully in your husband's confidence, perhaps you have some idea of who might have wanted to kill him?"

"It might have been anyone," she murmured, smiling disarmingly. "A jealous husband or lover. Such people do still exist, I believe."

"Did he ever receive threatening letters?"

"I don't think so. He had affairs with several of my friends, but I really don't see any of their husbands as murderers.

"Don't be misled, Chief Superintendent. My husband wasn't a heartless fiend. He was no coarse brute either, in spite of his looks.

"I daresay it will surprise you to hear me say so, but he was really very shy and insecure, which was why he was always having to bolster up his ego.

"And, you know, there's nothing more reassuring to a man than to know that he can have virtually any woman he wants."

"Were you always so tolerant?"

"At first he kept things from me. It took me years to find out that he'd been to bed with most of my women friends. It was only after I'd caught him in the act that we had it out once and for all, and since then we've been the best of friends.

"You do understand, don't you? In spite of everything, his death is a great loss. We were very fond of one another, and, anyway, old habits die hard."

"Was he a jealous husband?"

"He allowed me perfect freedom, but I realized that it would be an affront to his manhood to confide in him as he did in me. Where is his body now?"

"At the Forensic Laboratory. I'd be obliged if you could call there sometime tomorrow morning to make a formal iden-tification."

"Where was he hit?"

"In the chest and stomach."

"Did he suffer?"

"Death was almost instantaneous."

"Was the Grasshopper with him when he died?"

"No. He left before she did."

"So at the end he was quite alone."

"I'd be grateful if, sometime tomorrow, you would make out a list of all your women friends, and of any other women whom you know to have been your husband's mistresses."

"You're sure it was a man who shot him?"

"If Madame Blanche is to be believed, yes."

"Was the door left open, then?"

"No. She was watching through the small window. Thank you for your help, Madame Chabut, and please believe me when I say how sorry I am to have been the bearer of such distressing news. Incidentally, did your husband have any relatives living in Paris?"

"Only old Désiré, his father. He's seventy-three, but he still has his bistro at the Quai de la Tournelle. It's called 'Au Petit Sancerre.' He's a widower. He has a living-in housekeeper, a woman of about fifty."

Seated in the car, Maigret asked, turning to Lapointe:

"What do you think?"

"She's an odd sort of woman, isn't she? Do you think she was telling the truth?"

"I'm sure of it."

"She didn't seem much upset."

"That will come later. It will probably hit her in the night, as she lies alone in her bed. But if anyone sheds any tears, I daresay it will be the maid. There's no doubt in my mind that she was another of his conquests."

"He sounds like a nut case to me."

"You're probably right. But there are some like that, who have to keep proving to themselves that they really are men, just as his wife said. The Quai de la Tournelle, I think. . . . It's just possible that the bistro is still open."

They arrived just in time to see an old man with white hair, wearing a blue apron of coarse cotton, pulling down the iron shutter. Through the half-open door behind him, they could see the sawdust-covered floor of the bistro, tables with chairs stacked on them, and the zinc bar on which there were several dirty glasses.

"I'm sorry, gentlemen, we're closed."

"We just wanted a word with you."

He frowned.

"You want to talk to me? Who are you, may I ask?"

"Police. Criminal Investigation Department."

"I can't imagine what the Criminal Investigation Department can possibly have to say to me."

They were now inside the bistro. Désiré Chabut had shut the door. There was a large charcoal stove in one corner, and it was giving out a very good heat.

"It doesn't have to do with you. It's about your son."

He glowered at them mistrustfully. He looked like a regular peasant, with an expression in his eyes that was at once stolid and sly.

"My son? What's he done?"

"He hasn't done anything. He's met with an accident."

"I've always said he drives too fast. Is he badly hurt?"

"He's dead."

The old man said not a word, but went behind the bar, poured himself a small glass of marc brandy, and swallowed it down in one gulp.

"Would you like a glass?" he asked.

Maigret nodded, but Lapointe, who loathed marc brandy, refused.

"Where did it happen?"

"It wasn't a motor accident. Your son was shot with an automatic pistol."

"Who shot him?"

"That's what I'm trying to find out."

The old man, like the two women before him, showed no outward signs of grief. His furrowed face remained impassive, his eyes hard.

"Have you seen my daughter-in-law?"

"Yes."

"What did she say?"

"She doesn't know any more than we do."

"I've had this place for more than fifty years. Follow me."

He led the way into the kitchen, and switched on the light.

"You see that?"

He pointed to a couple of framed photographs of a little boy of about seven. In one he was carrying a hoop, and in the other, he was dressed up for his First Communion.

"That's him. He was born here, in the room upstairs. He went to the local school, and twice failed his *baccalauréat*. Then he got himself a job with a wine merchant as a door-to-door salesman. His employer was a winegrower from Mâcon, with a branch office in Paris. My son became his right-hand man in the end. Success didn't come all that easy to him, you can take my word for it. He worked hard. And when he got married, he barely earned enough to keep a wife."

"Did he love his wife?"

"Certainly he did. She was his boss's typist. To begin with, they lived in a couple of rented rooms on the Rue Saint-Antoine. They have no children. After a time, in spite of the fact that I did my best to dissuade him, Oscar decided to set up on his own. I was sure he'd burn his fingers, but not a bit of it, everything he touched turned to gold. You must have seen his barges on the Seine with *Vin des Moines* on the side in huge letters.

"You must understand that he could never have made such a success of it if he hadn't been very tough. As his business grew, a great many small businesses were forced into bankruptcy. It was no fault of his, of course, but, all the same, human nature being what it is, he made a lot of enemies."

"Are you suggesting that he was killed by one of his less fortunate competitors?"

"It seems the most likely explanation, don't you think?"

There was no mention of his son's mistresses, nor of the likelihood of his having been shot by a jealous husband or lover. Quite possibly Désiré knew nothing of these matters.

"Can you think of anyone in particular who might have had a grudge against him?"

"I can't give you their names, but there are such people. It might be worth your while making inquiries at the warehouses at Bercy. My son was generally regarded as a man who would not hesitate to ride roughshod over anyone who stood in his way."

"Did he come and see you often?"

"Hardly ever. In recent years we didn't see eye to eye on a number of things."

"Do you mean you didn't care for his business methods?"

"That, and other things. What does it matter now?"

Suddenly a tear, a single, solitary tear, spilled out of the corner of his eye and ran down his cheek. His hand shook a little, as he raised it to wipe away the tear with his forefinger.

"When can I see him?"

"Tomorrow, if you wish, at the Forensic Laboratory."

"That's somewhere near the center of town, across the river, isn't it?"

He refilled the two glasses, and gulped his down. He looked at the Chief Superintendent with glazed eyes. Maigret hurriedly emptied his glass. In the car, a few minutes later, he said:

"I'd be grateful if you'd drive me home. You'd better keep the car for tonight, and drive yourself home in it."

It was almost midnight when he climbed the stairs to his apartment. Before he was halfway up the door opened and his wife came out to meet him. He had telephoned her at eight, to say that he would be late. That was before the call from

Fourquet, when he had anticipated a protracted session with young Stiernet.

"You must be frozen."

"I've hardly put my nose out of doors all evening—just getting in and out of the car."

"You sound as if you've caught cold."

"My nose isn't running, and I haven't coughed once."

"Just you wait until morning. I'd better get you a hot grog, I think, and you can take a couple of aspirins with it. Has the boy confessed?"

All she knew was that Stiernet had battered his grandmother to death.

"No trouble at all. He didn't even attempt to deny it."

"Did he do it for money?"

"He was out of work. He'd just been turned out of his room because he owed three weeks' rent."

"What's he like? A brute?"

"No. His mental age is about six, I'd say. He doesn't really understand how it happened, and he has no conception of what's in store for him. He answers all the questions put to him to the best of his ability, attentively, like a kid in the classroom."

"Not responsible for his actions, do you think?"

"That's up to the judges. It's no concern of mine, thank heaven!"

"Will they appoint someone good for the defense?"

"A young man, making his first appearance at the Assizes, as usual. He hasn't a penny in the world, except three francs that were found in his pocket. It isn't because of him that I was kept so late. I was called out to another case. A middle-aged man, quite a well-known figure, was shot dead outside one of the most exclusive brothels in Paris."

"Won't be a moment. I can hear the kettle boiling. Your grog will be ready in a minute."

While she was in the kitchen, he undressed and got into his pajamas. Was it too late to smoke one last pipe before getting into bed? he wondered. Needless to say, he decided that it was not. Somehow, though, he did not relish it as much as usual. Could his wife possibly be right? Was he getting a cold?

# CHAPTER 2

When Madame Maigret came into the room with a cup of coffee in her hand and touched him on the shoulder, he was tempted, as he had often been when he was a child, to say that he didn't feel well and thought he'd better stay in bed and keep warm.

His head was throbbing, his sinuses were aching, and his forehead was damp. The windowpanes were milky white, like frosted glass.

He took a sip or two of coffee, then, with a groan, got out of bed and went to the window. A few early risers, their hands deep in their pockets, were hurrying toward the Métro. He could see them only in shadowy outline in the fog.

It was some time before he felt fully awake. He drank his coffee very slowly, and then lingered in the shower. It was not until he had finished shaving that his thoughts returned to Chabut.

He was fascinated by the man. Which of the people he had talked to had painted the truest picture of him?

To Madame Blanche, he was just a client, one of her best clients, admittedly, who never failed to order champagne when he was in her house. He needed to throw his money about, to display his wealth.

He must often have reflected:

"I started out as a door-to-door salesman. My father, who can barely read or write, still keeps a bistro on the Quai de la Tournelle."

And what did the Grasshopper really think of him? She had shed no tears. Even so, Maigret had had the feeling that she was not altogether indifferent to him. She knew that she was not the only woman he took to the plushy little private hotel on the Rue Fortuny, but she had shown no sign of jealousy.

The wine merchant's wife had shown still less. Maigret recalled one or two details that he had not consciously registered at the time. There was, for instance, the life-sized portrait in oils over the fireplace in the drawing room of the apartment on the Place des Vosges, a very glossy work, lifelike as a photograph. It portrayed Chabut with clenched fist, as though about to strike a blow, and a challenging expression in his eyes.

"How do you feel?"

"I'll be fine when I've had my second cup of coffee."

"All the same, you'd better have an aspirin, and stay indoors as much as you can. I'll phone for a taxi."

The wine merchant, still a somewhat shadowy figure in his mind, though he was gradually taking on shape and substance, accompanied him all the way to the Quai des Orfèvres. Maigret had the feeling that he had only to get to know Chabut to find his murderer.

The fog was still so thick that Maigret had to turn on the lights in his office. He opened his mail, signed a few interdepartmental notes, and then, seeing that it was nine o'clock, went off to the daily briefing in the Chief Commissioner's office.

When his turn came, he gave a summary of the case of Théo Stiernet.

"Is he mentally disturbed, would you say?"

"No doubt that's what his lawyer will plead, but in my opinion it's more a case of an unhappy childhood. The trouble is that he struck her fifteen times, so naturally there will be talk of bestial cruelty, especially as the old woman was his grandmother. He hasn't the faintest conception of what's in store for him. He does his best to answer all questions fully and truthfully, but he can't really see what all the fuss is about."

"And what about this Rue Fortuny business? There's just a brief mention, I see, in the morning papers."

"There'll be a great deal more before long, I'm afraid. The victim is a rich man, almost a public figure. You must have seen the *Vin des Moines* advertisements. They're plastered all over the Métro."

"A *crime passionnel*?"

"It's too early to say. If he wanted to make enemies, he certainly went about it the best way he could. There are a number of possibilities, and at this stage there's nothing to choose between them."

"Is it true that he was coming out of a house of assignation?"

"Is that what the papers are saying?"

"No, but I know the Rue Fortuny, and it wasn't difficult to put two and two together."

Maigret returned to his office, still brooding on the events of the previous night. Jeanne Chabut intrigued him almost as much as her husband. Undoubtedly, his death had been a shock to her, but even she had shed no tears over him.

She was, he would guess, five or six years younger than her husband. She had style. Where had she acquired that air of breeding which showed in her every gesture, in every inflection of her voice?

When they had first known one another, she had been a mere typist and he had not yet left the lean years behind him.

For all that Oscar went to the best tailors for his suits, he never lost his coarseness, and remained to the end something of a lout.

His rise had certainly been spectacular, but he had never quite got used to it, and had always felt the need to make a splash.

Apart from the absurdly pretentious portrait, the furniture and decorations of the apartment—a harmonious blend of the contemporary and the antique—must, Maigret felt sure, have been chosen by her. The whole atmosphere of the place induced a sense of well-being. About now, she would be getting ready to leave for the Forensic Laboratory, where the autopsy was probably already under way. She would go through the ordeal without flinching. A woman of her fiber would not be got down by the depressing atmosphere of what used to be known as the morgue.

"Are you there, Lapointe?"

"Yes, Chief."

"We're going out."

He struggled into his heavy overcoat, wound his scarf around his neck, and put on his hat. Before leaving the office, he paused to light his pipe. He and Lapointe got into one of the cars parked in the forecourt.

"Where to, Chief?"

"Quai de Charenton."

They drove along the Quai de Bercy, passing warehouse after warehouse, set back from the road behind iron railings. Each one bore a famous trade name in giant lettering. Three of the largest buildings were the warehouses of the Vin des Moines enterprises.

Farther on they came to an imposing wharf where dozens of wine casks were set out in rows, and others were being unloaded from a barge drawn up at the wharf. More of the Vin des Moines enterprises. More of Oscar Chabut's empire.

The building on the other side of the road was old and shabby, and surrounded by a huge area of featureless concrete. Here, too, there were vast numbers of wine casks. At the far end, open cases of wine in bottles were being loaded into trucks. A man with a drooping mustache and wearing blue overalls— some sort of foreman or supervisor, apparently—stood nearby.

"Shall I come in with you?"

"Yes, please."

"I'll just park the car."

Even out in the yard there was a pungent, winy smell. Maigret made for the nearest door, where an enamel plate invited callers to "Enter without ringing." The large tiled entrance hall was also redolent of wine.

On his left was a rather dark room with the door open, in which a girl with a slight squint sat at a telephone switchboard.

"What can I do for you?"

"Is Monsieur Chabut's private secretary in?"

She peered suspiciously at him.

"You mean you want to see her personally?"

"Yes."

"Do you know her?"

"Yes."

"Have you heard what's happened?"

"Yes. Tell her Chief Superintendent Maigret is here."

She gave him a searching look, then turned to young Lapointe, whom she clearly found more interesting.

"Hello! Anne-Marie? There's someone here who says he's Chief Superintendent Maigret. There's another man with him, I don't know his name. They want to see you. Yes. O.K. I'll send them up."

The staircase was thick with dust, and the walls could have done with a coat of fresh paint. On the stairs they passed a young man coming down, carrying a bundle of papers. The Grasshopper was waiting for them on the landing. She led them through an open door into an office which, though impressively large, was anything but luxurious.

It was dark and gloomy, and filled, like the courtyard and the rest of the building, with the sour smell of wine. To all appearances, the furniture and decorations had not been changed for fifty years.

"Have you seen her?"

"Who?"

"His wife."

"Yes. How well do you know her?"

"Sometimes, when he had the flu, I went to work at the Place des Vosges. She's a lovely woman, don't you think? And clever too. He set great store by her opinion, and would often ask her advice."

"This is a very dingy place, isn't it? I'm surprised."

"Wait till you see the offices on the Avenue de l'Opéra. They're very different. There they've got an illuminated *Vin des Moines* sign right across the building, and the offices are light and beautifully furnished, the last word in luxury. That's where they handle the sales end of the business. There are fifteen thousand outlets at present, and the number is going up every month. They have computers there and are almost entirely automated."

"And here?"

"These are the original offices. Nothing has changed here, and the provincial dealers like the old-world atmosphere. Chabut looked in every day at the Avenue de l'Opéra, but this is where he really felt at home."

"Did you go to the Avenue de l'Opéra with him?"

"Occasionally. Not very often. He had another secretary there."

"Apart from himself, who managed the business?"

"No one, really. He didn't trust anyone. Here, there's Monsieur Leprêtre. He's the head cellarman, in charge of production. Then, there's Monsieur Riolle, who keeps the books. He's only been with us a couple of months. And there are four typists in the room opposite."

"Is that all?"

"Except for the switchboard operator, whom you've already seen. And me, of course. It's hard to explain. You could say that this was General Headquarters, with most of the work being delegated to the Avenue de l'Opéra."

"How much time did he spend there, as a rule?"

"About an hour a day, sometimes two."

The old-fashioned roll-top desk was covered with papers.

"How old are the other typists? Young, like yourself?"

"Do you want to see them?"

"In time."

"One of them, Mademoiselle Berthe, is much older. She's thirty-two, and she's been here longer than the rest of us. The youngest is twenty-one."

"How did he come to engage you as his private secretary?"

"He was looking for a trainee. I saw the advertisement and applied for the job. That was about a year ago. I was not quite eighteen. I must have seemed a funny little thing to him. Anyway, he asked me whether I had a steady boy friend."

"Did you?"

"No. I had only just left secretarial school."

"When did he start making up to you?"

"He didn't 'make up to me,' as you put it. The very next day, he called me over, ostensibly to show me some papers, and started to caress me. He murmured something like 'I'll have to work this out.'"

"And then?"

"The following week, he took me to the Rue Fortuny."

"And what about the others? Weren't they jealous?"

"Well, you know, they'd all had their turn."

"Here?"

"Here or somewhere else. It's hard to explain. He was so open and natural about it, you couldn't hold it against him. I only know of one girl—she came after I did—who walked out on her third day, slamming the door behind her."

"How many people knew that your day was Wednesday?"

"Everyone, I should think. I always left with him and drove off in his car. He made no secret of it. Quite the contrary."

"Who had your job before you came?"

"Madame Chazeau. She's moved to the other office now. She's twenty-six, and divorced."

"Good-looking?"

"Yes. She has a lovely figure. No one could ever call her a grasshopper."

"No ill-feeling there?"

"I caught her looking at me with an odd sort of smirk once or twice at the beginning. I daresay she was thinking that I wouldn't last long."

"Was it all over between them?"

"I don't think so. She sometimes stayed on after office hours, and everyone knew what that meant."

"Was she at all embittered?"

"I never saw any sign of it. As I said, I rather got the impression that she was laughing at me. I'm quite used to not being taken seriously. Even my mother still treats me like a little girl."

"You don't think she might have wanted to get even with you?"

"She's not that sort. There are other men in her life. She goes out several nights a week, and the next day at work she can hardly keep her eyes open."

"What about the third girl?"

"Aline. She's the youngest, except for me. She's twenty-one, very dark, a bit temperamental. She makes a drama of everything. This morning she fainted, or pretended to, and the next thing she was crying her eyes out."

"Was she another of your predecessors?"

"Yes. She was working in one of the big stores when she saw the advertisement. They all came in answer to an advertisement."

"Do you think any one of them cared enough to take a shot at him?"

Madame Blanche, at the small window, had, so she said, seen the shadowy figure of a man between two parked cars. But might it not just as well have been a woman, a woman wearing trousers? It was dark at the time.

"That's not the way it was," replied the Grasshopper.

"What about his wife?"

"She wasn't jealous. She did as she pleased. As far as she was concerned, he was just a pleasant companion."

"Pleasant?"

She thought for a moment.

"When you got to know him, yes. At first sight, he seemed self-important, aggressive. He played the big boss. As far as women were concerned, he was always confident of success. When one got to know him better, one began to suspect that he was more naïve than he looked, and a good deal more vulnerable.

"He often asked, 'What do you really think of me?' especially after making love.

"I said, 'What should I think of you?'"

"'Do you love me? You don't. You might as well admit it.'"

"'It depends on what you mean by love. You make me feel good, if that's what you want to know.'"

"'What if I were to grow tired of you?'"

"'I don't know. I'd just have to put up with it, I suppose.'"

"'And the other girls across the way, what do they say?'"

"'Nothing. You know them better than I do.'"

"Tell me about the men," said Maigret.

"The men who work here, do you mean? Well, first of all, as I said, there's Monsieur Leprêtre. He used to have a business of his own, but he didn't have what it takes to make a success of it. He must be nearly sixty by now. He doesn't say much. He's very good at his job, and he gets on with it in his own quiet way."

"Is he married?"

"Yes. And he has two married children. He lives in a little house in Charenton, right at the end of the quay, and he bicycles to work every day."

Outside, the sun, veiled by the fog, filled the sky with a diffused pinkish glow, and vapor rose from the Seine. Lapointe, balancing his pad on his knee, was taking notes.

"When things went wrong for Leprêtre, was Le Vin des Moines already a going concern?"

"I think so, yes."

"What were his relations with Chabut?"

"His manner was deferential, and yet somehow one felt that he had his pride."

"Did they ever quarrel?"

"Not in my presence, and since I was nearly always there . . ."

"Am I right in thinking that he strikes you as being very reserved?"

"Reserved, and sad. I don't think I've ever seen him laugh, and besides, he has one of those drooping mustaches that give a man a rather pathetic air."

"Who else works in this building?"

"The accountant, Jacques Riolle. He's more of a cashier, really. He has his office downstairs. He only deals with some of the smaller accounts—we call them the petty cash transactions. It would take too long to explain all the detailed workings of the business. All the real accounting work is done at the Avenue de l'Opéra, as well as all the correspondence with the wholesalers. Here, our main concern is the buying side of the business. This is where the winegrowers from the South come on their periodic visits to Paris."

"Is Riolle in love with one of you girls?"

"If he is, he doesn't show it. You can judge for yourself. He's about forty, a confirmed bachelor, distinctly stuffy, a bit of an old maid really, timid, scared of his own shadow, always fussing over trifles. He lives in a family boardinghouse in the Latin Quarter."

"Anyone else?"

"Not in this building. Out there, in the storage sheds, there are five or six men. I know them by sight and by name, but, for all practical purposes, I have no contact with them whatever. I daresay you must find the whole setup rather odd, but if you'd known the boss you'd have thought it the most natural thing in the world."

"Will you miss him?"

"I won't deny it. Yes, I will."

"Did he give you presents?"

"He never gave me money. Once or twice he bought me a scarf that he'd taken a fancy to in a shop window."

"What will happen to the business now?"

"I don't know who will be taking charge. There is, of course, Monsieur Louceck, at the Avenue de l'Opéra. He's some sort of financial consultant. He and his team are responsible for the preparation and publication of balance sheets and so on. The trouble is he knows nothing about wine."

"And Monsieur Leprêtre?"

"As I said, he has no head for business."

"What about Madame Chabut?"

"I presume she'll inherit everything. I can't say whether she'll step into her husband's shoes. She might well be able to make a go of it. She's certainly a woman who knows what she wants."

Maigret looked intently at her. He was amazed to find a girl of her age so full of sound common sense, with a shrewd answer for every question. Her directness was very engaging, and he could not help smiling as he watched the gawky movements of her long, thin limbs.

"Last night, I went to the Quai de la Tournelle."

"To see the old man? Sorry, Monsieur Chabut's father, I should say."

"How did they get on?"

"From what I gathered, none too well."

"Why was that?"

"I don't know. I think it probably goes back a long way. In his father's eyes, I think, the son appeared unduly hard and insensitive. He steadfastly refused to accept anything from him, and if you ask me he's refused to retire, in spite of his age, just to annoy his son."

"Did Chabut ever talk about him?"

"Hardly ever."

"Can you tell me anything more?"

"No."

"Have you got any other lovers?"

"No. He was all I wanted."

"Will you stay on here?"

"If I'm allowed to."

"Where is Monsieur Leprêtre's office?"

"On the ground floor, overlooking the forecourt."

"I'll just look in across the way."

Here, too, the lights were on. Two of the girls were busy typing, and the third, the oldest, was filing letters.

"Don't let me disturb you. I'm the Chief Superintendent in charge of the case. Later, no doubt, I'll want to talk with each of you in turn. In the meantime, I should be glad to know whether any one of you has a possible suspect in mind."

They exchanged glances, and Mademoiselle Berthe, aged about thirty and rather plump, colored a little.

"Have you any ideas?" he asked her.

"No. I don't know a thing. I was taken completely by surprise, like everyone else."

"How did you hear about the murder? From the papers?"

"No. It was when I got here. . . ."

"Did he have any enemies, as far as you know?"

Once more they exchanged glances.

"There's no need to feel embarrassed. I already know a good deal about the sort of life he led and, in particular, his relations with women. It could have been a husband or lover, or a jealous woman."

There was no response. None of them seemed prepared to venture a comment.

"Think it over. Even the most trivial fact may be important."

He and Lapointe went down the stairs.

On the ground floor, following the Grasshopper's directions, Maigret opened the door of the accountant's office.

"Have you been with the firm for a long time?"

"Five months. Before that, I worked in a shop selling leather goods on the Grands Boulevards."

"Were you aware of your employer's amorous adventures?"

He flushed, opened his mouth as if to speak, but could find nothing to say.

"Among the people who came here to see him, was there anyone who had reason to hate him?"

"Why should anyone have hated him?"

"He drove a very hard bargain, didn't he?"

"He wasn't exactly softhearted."

No sooner were the words out of his mouth than he was regretting them. He should have known better than to express an opinion.

"Do you know Madame Chabut?"

"Occasionally she would bring in her personal bills for me to take care of, but usually they came by mail. She's a very friendly and unassuming person."

"Thank you."

Just one more, the melancholy Monsieur Leprêtre of the drooping mustache. They found him in his office, which was even shabbier and more provincial-looking than the rest of the building. He was sitting at a black-painted table, with a number of wine samples set out in front of him. His eyes, as he looked up at the two men, were full of mistrust.

"I suppose you know why we're here?"

He merely nodded. One end of his drooping mustache was longer than the other. He was smoking a meerschaum pipe, filled, if the smell was anything to go by, with a very strong tobacco.

"Someone must have had a very good reason for killing your employer. Have you worked here long?"

"Thirteen years."

"Did you get on with Monsieur Chabut?"

"I had no complaints."

"He had the fullest confidence in you, I take it?"

"He had no confidence in anyone but himself."

"Nevertheless, you were as close to him as anyone, surely?"

Leprêtre looked at him blankly. He was wearing a strange little skullcap, to conceal a bald patch, Maigret supposed. At any rate, he made no attempt to remove it.

"Is there nothing you can tell me?"

"Nothing."

"Did he ever mention having received threats?"

"No."

It was useless to persist, and Maigret beckoned Lapointe to follow him.

"Thanks."

"Don't mention it."

And Leprêtre got up and shut the door behind them.

It was not until they were in the car that Maigret's cold, which had been incubating since early morning, suddenly burst forth. For minutes on end he had to keep blowing his nose, so that his face grew flushed and his eyes watered.

"Sorry about that," he murmured to Lapointe. "It's been coming on since morning. Avenue de l'Opéra. I forgot to ask the number."

They had no difficulty in finding the building with the name *Vin des Moines* spread right across it in huge letters, which were illuminated at night. It was a massive and imposing edifice, in a row of similarly impressive buildings, flanked on one side by a foreign bank and on the other by a Trust Company.

They went up to the second floor, where they found themselves in a vast, marble-tiled hall with a very high ceiling. Chromium tables were dotted about here and there, with contemporary-style tubular steel chairs set out around them. Few of them were in use. On the walls were three immense posters, such as are to be found in the Métro, representing a jovial monk smacking his lips greedily over a glass of wine.

In each poster the wine was a different color—red, white, and rosé.

Behind a glass partition there was a huge office, in which some thirty people, men and women, were at work. Behind them was another glass partition, through which more offices could be seen. It was all very bright, and brilliantly lit, furnished and decorated in the very latest style.

Maigret went up to the reception desk, but before he could state his business he had to stop and blow his nose. The young receptionist waited, showing no sign of impatience.

"I beg your pardon. I wish to see Monsieur Louceck."

"Your name, please?"

She handed him a pad of slips on which were printed the words "Surname and Christian name," and underneath "Object of visit."

He wrote simply: "Chief Superintendent Maigret."

She disappeared through a door opposite the first partition and was gone some time. Eventually she returned by way of the front office and ushered them into a waiting room, somewhat cozier than the huge hall, but no less stylishly appointed.

"Monsieur Louceck won't keep you a moment. He's on the telephone."

And, as she had promised, they did not have long to wait. A second girl, wearing spectacles, led them into another spacious office. Here, too, everything was streamlined and contemporary in feeling.

A very small man rose from his chair and held out his hand.

"Chief Superintendent Maigret?"

"Yes."

"I am Stéphane Louceck. Do please sit down."

Maigret introduced his assistant:

"This is Inspector Lapointe."

"Take a seat, won't you?"

He was very ugly, in a rather repulsive way. His nose was long and bulbous, and streaked with bluish veins, and brown hair sprouted from his ears and nostrils. As to his eyebrows, they were almost an inch wide, and stood out like bristles. His suit needed pressing, and he was wearing a made-up tie that looked as if it were stiffened with whalebone.

"I presume it's about the murder."

"Needless to say, it is."

"I was expecting to hear from you before this. I never read the morning papers, my working day starts too early, so the first I knew of it was when Madame Chabut telephoned me."

"I didn't know of the existence of this office. We went first to the Quai de Charenton. I understand that that's where Oscar Chabut spent most of his time."

"He called in here every day. He was a man who liked to keep a personal eye on things."

His face was blank, without expression, and his voice flat and toneless.

"If you don't mind my asking, do you know if he had any enemies?"

"Not that I know of."

"He was a man of some power and influence. It seems likely that, on his way up, he must have trod hard on a few toes."

"I don't know anything about that."

"He had a great liking for women, I understand."

"His private life was no concern of mine."

"Which was his office?"

"This one. He shared this desk with me."

"Did he bring his private secretary with him?"

"No. We have all the staff we need here."

He did not attempt a smile, nor did he express even the most perfunctory regret at what had happened.

"How long have you been with the firm?"

"I was working for him long before these offices were built."

"What were you doing before that?"

"I was a financial consultant."

"I take it you are responsible for the accounts?"

"Among other things."

"Will you be taking over the business?"

Once more, Maigret blew his nose. He could feel beads of perspiration on his forehead.

"Excuse me."

"Take your time. I don't quite know how to answer your question. This isn't a public company. It's the personal property of Monsieur Chabut, so that, unless he has left it to someone else in his will, it passes automatically to his wife."

"Are you on good terms with her?"

"I scarcely know her."

"Would you describe yourself as Oscar Chabut's right-hand man?"

"I was in charge of sales and of the warehouses. We have more than fifteen thousand retail outlets up and down the country. Here, we have a staff of forty, and we have about twenty inspectors touring the provinces. There's a separate section on the floor above this to take care of Paris and the suburbs. They are also concerned with advertising and exports."

"How many women on your staff?"

"I beg your pardon?"

"I'm asking how many women and young girls you have on your staff."

"I don't know."

"Who engages them?"

"I do."

"Had Oscar Chabut no say in the matter?"

"Not in this department."

"Was he particularly attentive to any one of them?"

"Not that I am aware of."

"Would it be correct to say that the entire responsibility for the sales side of the business rests on your shoulders?"

At this he blinked, but made no reply.

"It seems likely, doesn't it, that you will be kept on here, and also invited to take charge at the Quai de Charenton?"

He sat motionless and impassive, his expression blank.

"Would any member of your staff have had cause for complaint against your employer?"

"I don't know."

"I take it you want to see the murderer arrested?"

"Of course."

"So far, you haven't been much help to me."

"I'm sorry."

"What is your opinion of Madame Chabut?"

"She's a very intelligent woman."

"Do you get on well with her?"

"You've already asked me that, and I've told you that I hardly know her. She scarcely ever set foot in this office, and I never went to the Place des Vosges. I don't go in for dinner parties and nights on the town."

"Did Chabut go in much for social life?"

"I couldn't say. You'd better ask his wife."

"Do you know if he left a will?"

"I've no idea."

Maigret's head was swimming. He realized that he was getting nowhere. Louceck had made up his mind to give nothing away, and he would maintain a stubborn silence to the bitter end.

The Chief Superintendent got up.

"I'd be obliged if you would draw up a list of all your staff, including ages and addresses, and let me have it as soon as possible at the Quai des Orfèvres."

Louceck, still imperturbable, merely gave a slight nod. He pressed a buzzer, and the door opened to admit a young woman, who promptly showed them out. Before getting back into the car, Maigret went into a bar and had a glass of rum, hoping that it might make him feel better. Lapointe had a fruit juice, to keep him company.

"What next?"

"It's nearly midday, too late to call at the Place des Vosges. We'll go back to the office and then have a bite to eat at the Brasserie Dauphine."

He went into the telephone booth and dialed the number of his apartment on the Boulevard Richard-Lenoir.

"Is that you? What's for lunch? No, I shan't be back. Keep it for my dinner tonight. I know I sound a bit hoarse. I've had a streaming nose for the past hour. See you this evening. . . ."

He was not in the best of moods.

"Almost anyone might have had a more or less compelling reason for wishing Chabut dead. But only one gave in to the temptation to shoot him. The others are innocent. All the same, innocent or not, you'd think they were all in a conspiracy to spike our guns, instead of helping us. With one exception, perhaps, the girl they call the Grasshopper. She's a funny kid, but all the same, she seems genuinely anxious to co-operate, and she doesn't weigh every word like the others. How does she strike you?"

"As you say, she's a funny kid. But she's not afraid of looking facts in the face, and she isn't easily taken in."

The medical report from the Forensic Laboratory was on Maigret's desk. It was more than four pages long and replete with technical terms. Appended were two diagrams showing the trajectory of the bullets. There were two in the abdomen, one in the chest, and a fourth just below the shoulder blade.

"No telephone messages?"

He turned to Lucas.

"Have you sent the report to the Public Prosecutor's Office?"

He was referring to the Stiernet case.

"First thing this morning. I've actually been down to see him in the cells."

"How is he?"

"Giving no trouble. He seems almost serene, really. He doesn't mind being locked up. You'd think he hadn't a care in the world."

A little while later, Maigret and Lapointe went across the street to the Brasserie Dauphine. At the bar there were two robed barristers, and also three or four inspectors. They were not in Maigret's Division, but they nevertheless greeted him respectfully. He and Lapointe went into the dining room.

"What's on today?"

"Your favorite, *blanquette de veau*."

"What's your opinion of Vin des Moines?"

The proprietor shrugged.

"It's no worse than the stuff that used to be sold by the liter in the old days. It's a mixture of wines from the South and from

Algeria. Nowadays, people prefer a label on their bottle, and the fancier the name, the better."

"Do you stock it?"

"Indeed I don't! What do you say to a drop of Bourgueil? Perfect with the *blanquette*."

Maigret was fumbling in his pocket for his handkerchief.

"Here we go again! As soon as I come into a warm room, it starts."

"Why don't you go home to bed?"

"What good would that do? It wouldn't stop me from worrying about that fellow Chabut. He's certainly making life difficult for us. You'd think he'd done it on purpose."

"What do you think of his wife?"

"I haven't made up my mind. Last evening she struck me as very charming and self-possessed, in the circumstances. A bit too self-possessed, maybe. As far as her relations with her husband are concerned, she seems to have been a kind of mother figure, protective and indulgent. Well, we'll see. I may change my mind after I've seen her again. I'm always a bit suspicious of these plaster saints."

The *blanquette* was tender and beautifully cooked, with a fragrant golden-yellow sauce. They each had a pear, followed by coffee, and shortly after two they entered the building on the Place des Vosges.

The door was opened by the maid whom they had seen the night before. She left them sitting in the hall and went to announce them to her mistress.

When she came back, she led them, not into the drawing room, but into a small sitting room beyond, where they were almost immediately joined by Jeanne Chabut.

She was wearing a very simple but beautifully cut black dress, with no jewelry of any kind.

"Do sit down, gentlemen. I was there this morning, and as a result I can't face the thought of lunch."

"I presume the body will be brought here?"

"At five this afternoon. The undertaker will be coming to see me first, to decide where to lay him out. It will be in here, no doubt. The drawing room is too big."

The little sitting room, with its huge window stretching almost from floor to ceiling, was light and colorful, like the rest of the apartment, but more distinctively feminine in character.

"Did you choose the furnishings?"

"I've always been interested in interior decorating. I should have liked to take it up professionally. My father has a bookshop on the Rue Jacob, not far from the Ecole des Beaux-Arts. That's where all the best antique shops are."

"What made you take up stenography?"

"I wanted my independence. I hoped I might be able to go to evening classes after work, but I soon realized that it couldn't be done. And then I met Oscar."

"Did you become his mistress?"

"From the very first evening. By now, that shouldn't surprise you."

"Was it he who proposed marriage?"

"Can you see it coming from me? I suppose he was getting fed up with living alone in a miserable little hotel, and cooking his meals on a spirit stove. He was very poor in those days."

"Did you go on working?"

"For the first two months. After that, he made me give it up. This may surprise you, but he was very jealous."

"Was he faithful?"

"So I believed."

Maigret watched her intently. There was something about her that had a false ring, and it made him uneasy. She had a lovely face, but her features were curiously set, almost as though she had undergone plastic surgery.

Her eyes, which were light blue and very large, were unblinking. Had she deliberately cultivated that air of wide-eyed innocence?

His nose was running again. She looked at him in silence, as he dabbed at it with his handkerchief.

"Excuse me."

"I've given some thought to that list you asked me for, and I've got down all the names I can think of. I didn't like doing it, but I've done it nevertheless."

She went across to a Louis XV desk and picked up a sheet of writing paper that was lying there. Her handwriting was large and firm, with no flourishes.

"I have included only those men whose wives I believe to have been on intimate terms with my husband."

"You're not sure about them?"

"In most cases, no. But, judging from the way he talked of them, and his manner toward them when we entertained them here, I'm pretty sure. It didn't take me long to recognize the signs."

In a low voice, he began reading out the names.

"Henri Legendre."

"He's an industrialist. He commutes between Paris and Rouen. Marie-France is his second wife. She's fifteen years younger than he is."

"Is he jealous?"

"I believe so, but she's one too many for him. They have a place at Maisons-Laffitte, where they have regular weekend house parties."

"Have you ever been?"

"Only once, because as a rule we had our own weekend house party at Sully-sur-Loire. We have a summer place at Cannes, too, the two top floors of a new building not far from Palm Beach. We have access to the roof, and I've made a garden up there. . . ."

"Pierre Merlot," he read.

"A stockbroker. Lucile, his wife, is a little blonde with a pointed nose. She's over forty, but she still affects the urchin look. That must have amused Oscar."

"Did her husband know?"

"I'm sure he didn't. He's a bridge fiend, and whenever we had people in he was always one of those shut up in here for a quiet rubber."

"Did your husband play?"

"No, bridge wasn't his particular game."

She smiled faintly.

"Jean-Luc Caucasson. He publishes art books. He married a young artist's model. She's pretty foulmouthed, but good fun all the same."

"Maître Poupard. Is that the criminal lawyer?"

He was one of the leading lights of the Bar, and his name often appeared in the newspapers. He was married to a very rich American woman.

"Did he suspect nothing?"

"He's often away from home on some case in the provinces. They have a magnificent apartment on the Ile-Saint-Louis."

"Xavier Thorel. The Cabinet Minister?"

"Yes. He's a delightful man, and a dear friend."

"You make it sound as though he was more your friend than your husband's."

"I'm very fond of him. As for Rita, she throws herself at every man she meets."

"Does he know?"

"He's resigned to it. Or rather, he gives as good as he gets."

More names, Christian names and surnames, an architect, a doctor, a famous dress designer on the Rue François Ier, and Gérard Aubin, partner in the bank of Aubin et Boitel.

"The list could have been longer, because we have a very wide circle of acquaintances, but I confined myself to those with whom I felt pretty sure Oscar was on intimate terms."

Changing the subject abruptly, she asked:

"Have you been to see his father?"

"Yes."

"What did he say?"

"I got the impression that he wasn't on the best of terms with his son."

"Only since Oscar started making a lot of money. He wanted his father to give up the bistro, and offered to buy him an attractive place at Sancerre, not far from where he was born. There was complete misunderstanding on both sides. Désiré thought we were trying to get rid of him."

"What about your own father?"

"He still has his bookshop and lives with my mother above the shop. She's completely housebound now. She has a weak heart, and has great difficulty in walking."

The maid knocked at the door and came in.

"The gentleman from the undertaker's is here."

"Tell him I'll be with him right away."

And, turning to the two men:

"I'll have to ask you to excuse me. I shall be kept terribly busy for the next few days. Still, if anything new crops up, or if I can be of any further use to you, don't hesitate to let me know."

She gave them a vague, somewhat mechanical smile and, leading the way with her graceful, fluid walk, showed them to the door.

In the hall they met the undertaker's man, who, recognizing Maigret, gave a respectful little bow.

The fog, which had almost cleared by lunchtime, was now beginning to thicken once more, and everything in the street looked a little blurred.

As to Maigret, he was blowing his nose again, and muttering heaven knows what imprecations under his breath.

# CHAPTER 3

**M**aigret was never altogether at ease with the aura of opulence that goes with certain reaches of the bourgeoisie. It made him feel awkward and out of place. For instance, all the people on the list that Jeanne Chabut had provided belonged more or less to the same set, with its own rules, customs, taboos, and private language. They forgathered in restaurants, theaters, and night clubs, spent their weekends together in country houses, and in the summer went off in droves to Cannes or Saint-Tropez.

Oscar Chabut, with his plebeian looks, had elbowed his way ruthlessly into this tight little world, and to prove to himself that he really had arrived he had found it necessary to go to bed with most of the women in it.

"Where to, Chief?"

"Rue Fortuny."

He was slumped in his seat, with glazed eyes, gloomily watching the streets and boulevards go by. The street lamps were lit, and there were lighted windows in most of the buildings. There were, besides, lights strung across the streets, with here and there little fir trees painted gold or silver, and, in the shop windows, glittering Christmas trees.

In spite of the cold and the fog, the streets were jammed with sightseers and shoppers, gazing in shop windows and crowding into the stores. He wondered what he should give Madame Maigret for Christmas, but he saw nothing that appealed to him. He blew his nose incessantly and longed to get home and to bed.

"When we've finished at the Rue Fortuny I'll give you the list and leave you to find out where they all were around nine on Wednesday night."

"Am I to ask them myself?"

"Only if you can't find out any other way. In most cases, I think, you'll be able to get the information from the servants or the chauffeur."

Poor Lapointe was not exactly overjoyed at the prospect.

"Do you think it's one of them?"

"It could be anyone. Our friend Oscar seems to have gone out of his way to make himself universally detested, at least as far as the men were concerned. You can wait for me in the car. I won't be more than a few minutes."

He rang the bell of Madame Blanche's house. He had not heard the sound of approaching footsteps, but the little window opened and Madame Blanche came to the door, though with obvious reluctance, to let him in.

"What do you want now? This is my busiest time, and I don't want my clients disturbed by policemen tramping all over the house."

"I want you to take a look at this list of names."

They were alone in the great reception room, lit only by two shaded table lamps. Having looked about for her spectacles, and found them on the grand piano, she glanced through the list.

"What do you want to know?"

"Whether there are any clients of yours on this list."

"First of all, as I've already told you, I only know my clients by their first names. Surnames are never mentioned here."

"Knowing you, I haven't the least doubt that you've made it your business to find out all you can about them."

"People like myself are in a position of trust, in the same way as doctors and lawyers, and I don't see why we shouldn't be entitled to the privilege of professional secrecy, just as they are."

He listened patiently, then said quietly:

"I'm afraid I shall have to insist on an answer."

"There are two or three."

"Who are they?"

"Monsieur Aubin, Gérard Aubin, the banker. He's one of a powerful group of Protestant financiers, and he goes to great lengths to protect his reputation."

"Does he come often?"

"Two or three times a month."

"Does he bring his companion with him?"

"No, she always arrives first."

"Always the same one?"

"Yes."

"Has he ever run into Chabut in the hall or on the stairs?"

"I take very good care to see that doesn't happen."

"He could have seen him entering or leaving the house, or recognized his car. What about his wife? Has she ever been here?"

"Yes, with Monsieur Oscar."

"Who are the others?"

"Marie-France Legendre, the industrialist's wife."

"Did she come often?"

"Four or five times."

"Also with Chabut?"

"Yes. I don't know her husband. If he's ever been here, it was under an assumed name. Some prefer it that way. The Minister,

Xavier Thorel, for instance. He calls me up in advance, to give me time to find a young woman for him, preferably a fashion model or a cover girl. He calls himself Monsieur Louis, but his photograph often appears in the papers, so everyone knows who he is."

"Do any of them come regularly on Wednesdays?"

"No, they haven't any special day."

"Was Madame Thorel one of Oscar Chabut's mistresses?"

"Rita? She came with him once or twice, but he was by no means the only one. She's a provocative little brunette, and she can't do without men. I don't mean she's a nymphomaniac. It's just that she has to be the center of attention."

"Thank you."

"Will that be all?"

"I don't know, at this point."

"Do me a favor: next time you come, give me a ring first. You must understand that if you were seen in this house by the wrong people, it could do me a lot of harm. I'm grateful to you, at any rate, for not having given my name to the reporters."

Maigret returned to his car. He was not much further forward, but, in the absence of any real lead, he could not afford to leave any stone unturned.

"Where to now, Chief?"

"Home."

His forehead was hot, his eyes were smarting, and he was troubled by an ache in his left shoulder.

"Courage, man. You've got the list, haven't you? To start with, you'd better go back to the Quai and have a photostat copy made. We don't want to have to bother Jeanne Chabut again."

Madame Maigret was amazed to see him back so much sooner than usual.

"It looks to me as though you've got a shocking cold. That's why you're home so early, I suppose."

He was sweating profusely.

"It wouldn't surprise me if I were in for a bout of flu. It could hardly have come at a worse time."

"It's a queer business, isn't it?"

Most of the time, as in this instance, she knew no more about Maigret's cases than she could read in the newspapers or hear on the radio.

"Hold on a minute. I've got to make a phone call."

He called the Rue Fortuny and heard Madame Blanche's bland voice on the line.

"Maigret speaking. There's one thing I forgot to ask you, just now. Did Chabut let you know by telephone when he was coming?"

"Sometimes he did, sometimes not."

"Did he telephone on Wednesday?"

"No. There wasn't any point. He almost always came on Wednesdays."

"Who knew that, besides yourself?"

"No one here."

"What about your maid?"

"She's Spanish—very young. She hardly speaks a word of French, and she can't catch people's names, let alone remember them. . . ."

"Nevertheless, someone must have known, the person who knew roughly what time Chabut would be leaving your house, and was waiting for him outside, in spite of the freezing weather."

"I'm sorry, I'll have to hang up. There's someone at the front door."

He undressed, got into his pajamas and dressing gown, went back into the sitting room, and slumped into his leather armchair.

"Your shirt is soaked through. You'd better take your temperature."

She brought the thermometer from the bathroom and made him keep it in his mouth for a full five minutes.

"Well?"

"A hundred and two.

"Why don't you go straight to bed? Don't you think it would be as well for me to ask Pardon to look in on you?"

"It would be a fine thing if he were called out every time one of his patients had a mild attack of flu!"

He hated bothering the doctor, especially when it was his old friend Pardon, who seldom managed to get through a meal without interruptions.

"I'll go and turn down the bed."

"Hold on a minute. Did you keep that *choucroute* for me?"

"You surely don't want it now?"

"Why not?"

"It's so indigestible. You're not well."

"Warm it up for me anyway, and don't forget the pickled pork."

It all turned on one crucial point. Someone had known that Chabut would go to the Rue Fortuny that Wednesday evening. It was unlikely that the murderer had followed him. In the first place, it was no easy matter to follow anyone in Paris, especially if he was in a car. In the second place, it had been seven o'clock or thereabouts when the wine merchant had arrived, together with the Grasshopper.

Was it conceivable that the murderer should have hung about for the best part of two hours in freezing weather, and that no one should have noticed him? And another thing, he had obviously not come by car, since, as soon as he had fired the shots, he had rushed off to the Malesherbes Métro station.

His head was fairly spinning. He really must pull himself together and think.

"What will you have to drink?"

"Beer, of course. What else would go with *choucroute?*"

Much as he had been looking forward to the *choucroute*, when it came he could manage no more than a mouthful or two, then he quickly pushed his plate aside. It was unheard of for him to go to bed at half past six in the evening. Nevertheless, he did so. Madame Maigret brought him two aspirins.

"What else can I give you? Last time, I seem to remember— it must have been about three years ago—Pardon gave you a bottle of something that did you a lot of good."

"I don't remember."

"Seriously, don't you think I should give him a ring?"

"No. Draw the curtains and put out the light."

Within ten minutes, he was perspiring freely. His thoughts began to drift, and in a little while he fell asleep.

But it was to be a long night. Several times he woke, with his nasal passages blocked, gasping for breath. It was not easy to get back to sleep. For a while he lay in a half-conscious doze and, in this state, kept imagining he heard his wife's voice.

Then he saw her, standing beside the bed, with a pair of clean pajamas over her arm.

"You'll have to change. You're sopping wet. I wonder if I shouldn't change the sheets too."

He let her do as she wished, only dimly conscious of what was happening. Later, he found himself inside a church, which reminded him, on a much larger scale, of Madame Blanche's reception room. All down the center aisle there were couples, seemingly queuing up to get married. Someone was seated at a piano, but the music that filled the church was that of an organ.

There was something he had to do, but he could not remember what it was, and out of the corner of his eye he could see

Oscar Chabut sneering at him. As each couple filed past him, he spoke to the woman by her Christian name.

At last, half awake, Maigret saw the gray light of morning creeping into the bedroom and caught the smell of coffee coming from the kitchen.

"Are you awake?"

He was no longer sweating. He felt drained and languid, but otherwise quite comfortable.

"Is my coffee ready?"

He could not remember when he had last enjoyed a cup of coffee so much. He drank in little sips, savoring it.

"Hand me my pipe and tobacco, will you? What's the weather like?"

"A bit misty, but not nearly as bad as yesterday. I think the sun will be out shortly."

Not often, but once or twice in his childhood, he had made himself ill because he had not managed to finish his homework. Had this cold of his been just such a psychological indisposition? Surely not, since he had actually had a temperature.

Before giving him his pipe, Madame Maigret handed him the thermometer. Obediently, he slid it under his tongue.

"Ninety-eight degrees. Below normal."

"No wonder, considering the way you've been perspiring."

He smoked his pipe, drank another cup of coffee.

"You'll give yourself at least one day's rest, I hope."

He did not reply immediately. He had not made up his mind. He felt very comfortable, lying in his warm bed, especially now that he no longer had a headache. Lapointe was hard at work, checking the alibis of all the men on the list.

The case was hanging fire. It was disheartening, the more so because he somehow felt himself to blame. The key to the mystery was within his grasp, if only he could put his hand on it.

"Anything new in the papers?"

"They say you're on the track of someone."

"Which is exactly the opposite of what I told them!"

By nine o'clock he had drunk three large cups of coffee, and the air in the bedroom was blue with the fumes of his pipe.

"What do you think you're doing?"

"I'm getting up."

"You're not going out, are you?"

"Yes."

Knowing that it would be useless, she did not protest.

"Would you like me to call the Quai and ask them to send an inspector with a car?"

"Good idea. Lapointe won't be there. See if Janvier is available. No, on second thoughts, he's on another case. But Lucas could probably manage it."

He did not feel quite so well, out of bed. His head was swimming a little, and when he shaved his hand shook and he gave himself a slight cut.

"You'll be back for lunch, I hope? It won't do anyone any good to have you seriously ill."

She was right, of course, but he could not help himself. His wife wound his thick scarf around his neck and stood on the landing, watching him as he went down the stairs.

"Good morning, Lucas. The boss hasn't been asking for me, has he?"

"I told him you weren't feeling too good last night."

"Anything new?"

"Lapointe was out all evening with his list, and he was off again the first thing this morning. Where would you like me to take you?"

"Quai de Charenton."

He was already beginning to feel at home there. He went straight upstairs, followed by Lucas, who, not having been there before, was looking about him at the dingy walls. He knocked at the door, and went in, to find the Grasshopper at her desk, typing.

"It's me again. This is Inspector Lucas, my oldest colleague."

"You look tired."

"I am. I have several important questions, one in particular, to ask you."

He sat down in Chabut's chair, behind the roll-top desk.

"Who knew that your employer was always to be found on the Rue Fortuny on Wednesdays?"

"Among the people here, do you mean?"

"Here or elsewhere."

"Everyone here knew. Oscar was nothing if not indiscreet. The minute he made a new conquest, he had to let everyone know."

"Were you used to leaving the office at the same time as he did?"

"Yes, and I drove off in the car with him. It was all perfectly obvious."

"And this took place every Wednesday, more or less?"

"More or less, yes."

"Did Monsieur Louceck know?"

"I couldn't say. He scarcely ever came here. The boss was there every day, on the Avenue de l'Opéra, and he usually stayed for an hour or two."

"Can you give me some idea of his usual timetable?"

"Well, it varied, of course, but let's take an average day. He would leave home at about nine in the morning, driving the Jaguar. He had a chauffeur, to drive the Mercedes, but that was mostly for his wife's use. He usually called in first at the Quai de Bercy, just to keep an eye on things. That's where the wines are blended and bottled. . . ."

"Who's in charge there?"

"Nominally, Monsieur Leprêtre. He goes there from time to time, but there is also a sort of assistant manager on the spot. He comes from Sète originally, I believe."

"Does he ever come here?"

"Very rarely."

"Does he know of your relations with your employer?"

"I shouldn't wonder but that he's heard the gossip."

"Has he ever shown any particular interest in you?"

"I doubt if he's even noticed me."

"I see. Well, go on."

"Monsieur Chabut would get here at about ten, and go through his mail. If he had any engagements fixed for that day, I reminded him of them. Usually, one or two wholesalers from the South would call in to see him during the course of the morning."

"What was his attitude to you, during working hours?"

"It varied. Sometimes he'd scarcely notice I was there. At other times he'd say, 'Come here,' and hitch up my skirt, and make love to me on the edge of the desk. He never bothered to lock the door."

"Were you ever caught in the act?"

"A couple of times, by one of the typists, and once by Monsieur Leprêtre. It was no surprise to the girls, they'd had the same experience themselves."

"What time did he leave?"

"If he was lunching at home, about midday. If he had a lunch appointment in town, as he often did, he would leave at about half past twelve."

"Where do you have lunch?"

"A couple of hundred yards from here, on the Quai. There's a little restaurant where the food isn't at all bad."

"What about the afternoon?"

Lucas, worthy soul that he was, was listening to all this in amazement, and looking the Grasshopper up and down, as though he couldn't make her out at all.

"Almost every day he went on to the Avenue de l'Opéra, where he generally stayed until about four. He shared an office with Monsieur Louceck."

"Did he carry on with the girls there, too?"

"I don't think so. It's a different world. The atmosphere isn't the same at all. Besides, I suspect he wouldn't have had the nerve, with Monsieur Louceck around. Strange as it may seem, he was a bit scared of him, I think. Well, perhaps scared is too strong a word. At any rate, he treated him differently from the others, and as far as I know he never raised his voice to him."

"So he'd be back here soon after four?"

"Between four and half past. He would usually spend some time with Monsieur Leprêtre, and occasionally he would go down to the wharf to watch a barge being unloaded. Then he'd come up here, ring for a typist, and dictate letters."

"Wasn't that your job?"

"No. I only dealt with his personal correspondence. What he really needed was someone about the office, someone who didn't matter, with whom he could think aloud. That was my job. It wouldn't have made any real difference if I'd done no work at all."

"What time did he leave?"

"Six, as a rule, except when he felt like staying on with me, or one of the other girls."

"Did he never spend a whole evening with you?"

"Only on Wednesdays, till about nine."

"Did you always stay behind at Madame Blanche's?"

"No, sometimes we left together, and he drove me home to the Rue Caulincourt. He always dropped me about a hundred yards from my front door. Last Wednesday he was in a hurry, so I said not to wait for me."

"I'd like you to give this a little more thought. Try to think of anyone else who might have known about your visits to the Rue Fortuny."

He blew his nose and put on his hat. Madame Maigret had been right. The sun had come out and was casting glittering reflections on the Seine.

"Thanks, Mademoiselle. Come, Lucas."

As the car was turning into the forecourt of Police Head-quarters, Maigret caught a glimpse of a man standing near the parapet of the Quai. It was no more than a glimpse, and the Chief Superintendent thought nothing of it at the time, especially as, almost at once, the man made off toward the Place Dauphine, limping a little.

Later he said to Lucas:

"Did you spot him?"

"Who?"

"The man in the gabardine raincoat. He was across the street, watching the entrance and looking up at the windows. As we drove past, he looked me straight in the eye. I'm sure he recognized me."

"A tramp?"

"No, he was clean-shaven and decently dressed, though I'd scarcely have thought this was the weather for a gabardine coat."

When he got to his office, Maigret still had the unknown man on his mind. Mechanically, he crossed to the window and looked out. Needless to say, he was no longer there, on the Quai.

He tried to recall what it was about the man that had struck him so forcibly. Perhaps it was the intensity of his gaze, he thought. There had been something pathetic about him, as though he were faced with a grave problem, or in the throes of some deep personal unhappiness.

Maigret could almost have believed that he had seen a direct appeal for help in his eyes.

He shrugged, filled his pipe, and sat down at his desk. Every now and again, for no apparent reason, he broke out in a sweat, and had to mop his face with his handkerchief.

He had promised Madame Maigret that he would be home to lunch, but he had forgotten to ask her what they would be having. He always liked to know before he went out in the morning. It gave him something to look forward to.

The telephone rang, and he picked up the receiver.

"I have a call for you, sir, but the caller refuses to state his name or business. Do you wish to speak to him, even so?"

"Put him through. Hello . . ."

"Chief Superintendent Maigret?" the caller asked, in a somewhat muffled voice.

"Speaking."

"I have just one thing to say: Don't lose any sleep over the wine merchant. He was a lousy swine."

"Did you know him well?" Maigret asked, but the caller had already hung up. Slowly Maigret replaced the receiver, and he remained gazing thoughtfully at the instrument. This, perhaps, was what he had been waiting for since the start of the case: a real lead at last.

Admittedly, he had learned nothing from the caller, except that someone, somewhere in this business—the murderer, more likely than not—was one of those people who could not endure being completely ignored. Such people usually wrote anonymous letters, or telephoned. They were not necessarily all madmen or cranks.

He had encountered this sort of thing once or twice before. In one case, the guilty man had given him no peace until he had arrested him.

With an aching head, he opened his mail, signed a number of reports, and dealt with various administrative matters, which always seemed to him to take up just as much of his time as the actual conduct of an investigation.

At midday he left the office. He walked as far as the entrance to the Law Courts, then, after a moment's hesitation, went into the café on the corner. His mouth felt dry, and he needed a drink. Having had a glass of rum the night before, he decided to order the same again. Actually, he ordered two. They were very small glasses.

He went home in a taxi and, rather slowly, climbed the stairs. He had barely reached the landing when his wife opened the door and, taking a good look at him, asked:

"How are you feeling?"

"Better. Except that every now and then I break out in a sweat. What's for lunch?"

He removed his coat, hat, and muffler and went into the living room.

"Calves' liver *à la bourgeoise*."

It was one of his favorite dishes. He sat down in his armchair and glanced absent-mindedly through the newspapers.

Could it be that the mysterious caller was the same man whom he had noticed a short while before on the Quai, opposite the entrance to Police Headquarters?

He would have to wait for him to telephone again. He might even call him up here at home. His apartment on the Boulevard

Richard-Lenoir was always being mentioned in the papers. Besides, every taxi driver in Paris knew his address.

"What's on your mind?" asked Madame Maigret, as she set the table.

"I caught a glimpse of a man earlier today. Our eyes met, and I had the feeling that he was trying to convey some sort of message to me."

"With a look?"

"Why not? Not long afterward, a man telephoned me just to tell me that Chabut was a lousy swine. Those were his exact words. I don't know if it was the same man. He hung up before I had a chance to find out."

"Are you hoping he'll telephone again?"

"Yes. They nearly always do. They get a kick out of playing with fire. Unless, of course, it's just some unfortunate crank, who knows no more about the case than he's read in the newspapers. I've had a few of those, too."

"You don't want the television on, do you?"

They ate almost in silence. Maigret's mind, needless to say, had reverted to the case and the people involved.

"Have you had enough? If you have, we'll have the rest cold as a first course tomorrow."

If anything, he preferred calves' liver cold, after it had stood for a day. For dessert, he cracked a few walnuts and almonds, and ate them with a couple of figs. He had had only two glasses of claret with his meal. All the same, he felt drowsy. He got up from the table and slumped down in his armchair by the window.

He closed his eyes and dozed for some considerable time on the brink of sleep. He could feel himself drifting into sleep. It was a pleasant sensation, and he had no wish to dispel it.

And there, before his eyes, was the man whom he had seen
on the Quai, the man with a slight limp. Was it in his left foot
or his right? Half asleep as he was, the question assumed an
importance that he would have been hard put to it to justify if
he had been fully awake.

Madame Maigret cleared the table, going back and forth to
the kitchen noiselessly. Had he not felt a slight current of air
from time to time, he would not have known she was there.

Gradually, he ceased to be aware of his surroundings. His
mouth, though he did not know it, had fallen open, and he was
snoring gently. He woke with a sudden start, surprised to find
that he was in his own armchair. He glanced up at the clock.
It was five past three. He looked about for his wife. A slight
swishing sound from the kitchen told him that she was in there,
ironing.

"Did you have a good nap?"

"Marvelous. I could have slept all day."

"Won't you take your temperature?"

"If you want me to."

This time it was a hundred degrees.

"Do you have to go back to the office?"

"I'm afraid so, yes."

"You'd better have an aspirin first."

Obediently, he took one, then, to get rid of the taste, he poured
himself a small tot of sloe gin from the bottle his sister-in-law
had sent them from Alsace.

"I'll phone for a taxi right away."

Although the sky was clear and blue, a rather pale blue, and
the sun was shining, it was still very cold.

"Shall I turn the heater on, sir? You look as if you have a cold.
My wife and kids are all down with flu. When one gets it, we
all get it. It will be my turn next, I daresay."

"Thanks, but I'm better off without the heater. I keep breaking out in a sweat as it is."

"You too? I've been soaked through three or four times today already."

The stairs seemed steeper than usual, and it was a relief, when he finally reached his office, to sit down at his desk. He rang and asked for Lucas.

"Nothing new?"

"Nothing at all, Chief."

"No anonymous phone calls?"

"No. Lapointe has just got back. He's waiting to see you, I think."

"Send him in."

He took a pipe from the rack on his desk, the smallest one, and filled it slowly.

"Were you able to get all the information we needed?"

"More or less, yes. Luck was on my side."

"Sit down. Let's see the list."

"You won't be able to read my notes. If you don't mind, I'll read them out to you, and later I'll let you have a full report. To start with the Minister, Xavier Thorel, I didn't have to ask any questions. I found out from Thursday's papers that he was representing the Government that night at the world première of a film about the Resistance."

"With his wife?"

"Yes, Rita was there too, and their eighteen-year-old son."

"Go on."

"It struck me that there might be others on the list who had also attended the première but weren't important enough to get their names in the papers. And, in fact, one of them was, a Dr. Rioux, who lives on the Place des Vosges, only a couple of doors away from the Chabuts."

"How did you find out?"

"Simple. I asked the concierge. Perhaps not the most up-to-date method of gathering information, but still the best. It seems that Madame Chabut is Dr. Rioux's patient."

"Is she often ill?"

"Well, she sends for him fairly often, it seems. He's rather a fat man, with a few sparse brown hairs, which he brushes carefully over his bald patch. His wife is a big horsy redhead, not at all Oscar Chabut's type, I'd guess."

"That's two of them. Go on."

"Henri Legendre, the industrialist, was in Rouen, where he has a *pied-à-terre*. He usually spends one or two nights a week there. I got all this from his chauffeur, who mistook me for an insurance salesman."

"What about his wife?"

"She's been in bed for a week with flu. I couldn't get anything definite on the stockbroker, Pierre Merlot. He's said to have been dining out with his wife Lucile, which apparently he often does. It seems he's something of a gourmet, so I shall do the rounds of the best restaurants as soon as I can. That should produce something."

"What about Caucasson, the art-book publisher?"

"He was at the movie on the Champs-Elysées, same as the Minister."

"And Maître Poupard?"

"He was one of dozens being entertained at dinner by the American Ambassador on the Avenue Gabriel."

"What about Madame Poupard?"

"She was there too. Then there's a Madame Japy, Estelle Japy, widowed or divorced. She lives alone on the Boulevard Haussmann. Apparently, she was Chabut's mistress for years.

To find out about her, I had to make up to her maid. She hasn't seen Chabut for months, and I gather he treated her very shabbily. On Wednesday she was alone for dinner and spent the rest of the evening looking at television."

Maigret's telephone rang. He picked up the receiver.

"A personal call for you, sir. I think it's the same man who telephoned this morning."

"Put him through."

There was a long silence, during which he could hear the breathing of the caller.

At last the man spoke:

"Are you there?"

"Yes, I'm listening."

"It's only to tell you again that he was a lousy swine. Never lose sight of that."

"Hold on a minute."

But the man had already hung up.

"He could be the murderer, but he could just as well be a practical joker. As long as he keeps hanging up on me, I've no way of finding out. There's no way to trace him, either. We can only hope that he'll drop his guard and say too much, or do something silly."

"What did he say?"

"The same as he said this morning: that Chabut was a lousy swine."

No doubt there were a great many people in Chabut's circle who shared this view. He had done everything possible to get himself disliked, if not hated, both in his pursuit of women and in his conduct toward his staff.

It almost looked as if he had deliberately set out to provoke animosity. Yet until last Wednesday no one, as far as was known, had ever attempted to put him in his place. Had he ever had his face slapped? If so, he had kept it very dark. Had anyone ever, in a fit of jealousy, hit him on the jaw?

He had been overwhelmingly arrogant, so sure of himself that he had not shrunk from tempting Providence over and over again.

But in the end someone, a man according to Madame Blanche, had had enough, and had lain in wait for him outside the house on the Rue Fortuny. This man must have had an even more compelling reason than the rest for hating him, since he had been prepared to risk his liberty, if not his life, by killing him.

Was it among Chabut's friends that this man was to be found? The results of Lapointe's inquiries had been, on the whole, disappointing. Matrimonial infidelity scarcely ever ended in murder nowadays, especially in the circles in which Chabut moved.

Was the murderer one of the employees at the Quai de Charenton? Or at the Avenue de l'Opéra?

And was he or was he not the nameless man who had twice telephoned the Chief Superintendent, in order to unburden himself?

"Have you been through the whole list with me?"

"Just a couple more names: Philippe Borderel and his mistress. He's a theater critic on one of the leading dailies. He was at a dress rehearsal at the Théâtre de la Michodière. Then there's Trouard, the architect. He was dining at Lipp's with a client, name unknown."

How many more people, not on the list, had good cause to bear a grudge against the wine merchant? The only way to find out was to interview scores of men and women, one by one, face to face. And that, needless to say, was just not possible, which was why Maigret set so much store by the unknown man who had telephoned him, and who might or might not be the same man whom he had seen standing near the parapet that morning.

"When is the funeral, do you know?"

"No. The undertaker's men had just arrived as I was leaving Madame Chabut. The body should have been taken to the Place des Vosges late yesterday afternoon. Come to think of it, perhaps we might go along there and have a look."

A few minutes later they were in the car, on their way to the Place des Vosges. The door to the first-floor apartment was open. They went in and were at once assailed by a strong smell of chrysanthemums and candle wax.

Oscar Chabut was lying in an open coffin, with the lid beside it. Kneeling at the prie-dieu was an elderly woman dressed in deep mourning, and a youngish couple stood nearby, looking at the dead man, whose face was illuminated by the flickering candles.

Who was the old woman in mourning? Jeanne Chabut's mother? It was certainly possible, indeed probable. The young couple seemed very ill at ease. The man took his companion by the elbow and, after they had both crossed themselves, led her out.

Maigret, following custom, took the little sprig of rosemary from the bowl of holy water and made a sign of the cross with it over the coffin. Lapointe followed suit with such fervor that Maigret could not help smiling to himself.

Even in death, Oscar Chabut was impressive. Coarse-featured though he was, his face was strong and endowed with a strange kind of beauty.

As the two men were leaving they came face to face with Madame Chabut in the hall.

"Were you wanting to see me?"

"No. We came to pay our last respects to your husband."

"You'd think he was alive, wouldn't you? They've done a marvelous job on him. You've seen him now, exactly as he was in life, except, alas, for the expression in his eyes." Like an automaton, she led them across the hall to the front door.

Abruptly, Maigret murmured:

"There's something I should like to ask you, Madame."

She looked at him with interest.

"I'm listening."

"Do you really want your husband's murderer found?"

It was so unexpected that, for a moment, she could not get her breath.

"Why ever should I want that man, of all men, to go free?"

"I don't know. If he's found, there will be a trial, a sensational trial, with full coverage by the press, radio, and television. What's more, a great many public figures will be called as witnesses. Your husband's employees will also have to give evidence. Some of them, at least, will tell the truth. Maybe some of your husband's friends will, too."

"I see what you mean," she murmured thoughtfully, as though she were weighing up the pros and cons.

After a brief pause, she added:

"There'll be a colossal scandal!"

"You haven't answered my question."

"To be honest, I don't care one way or the other. I'm not out for revenge. I don't doubt that the man who killed him thought he had good cause for what he did. Maybe he really had. What good would it do anyone to lock him up for ten years, or even for the rest of his life?"

"In other words, if you had some inkling of who he was, you'd keep it to yourself?"

"As I have no such inkling, that's a hypothetical question. If I had, it would be my duty to tell you, wouldn't it? And I believe I should do so, however unwillingly."

"Who is going to take over your husband's business? Louceck?"

"That man frightens me. He's a cold-blooded fish, and I can't bear to feel his eyes on me."

"Still, your husband seems to have trusted him."

"Louceck coined money for him. He's very shrewd. He knows every law in the book, and how to get around it. In the beginning he was merely my husband's tax consultant, but he gradually worked his way up, until he was his right-hand man."

"Who founded Vin des Moines?"

"My husband. The business was run entirely from the Quai de Charenton in those days. It was Louceck who advised Oscar to open an office on the Avenue de l'Opéra and to set up more warehouses in the provinces, so as to increase the retail outlets."

"In your husband's opinion, was he honest?"

"Oscar needed him. And he was able to stand up for himself."

"You haven't answered my question. Will he be running the business?"

"He'll go on as at present, no doubt, at least for a time, but he won't rise any higher."

"Who will be the boss?"

"I will."

She said this quite simply, as though anything else was inconceivable.

"I've always been a businesswoman at heart. My husband often turned to me for advice."

"Will you have your office on the Avenue de l'Opéra?"

"Yes, but I won't share it with Louceck, as Oscar did. There's plenty of space."

"And will you supervise the warehouses, and the cellars and offices at the Quai de Charenton?"

"Why shouldn't I?"

"Are you thinking of making any staff changes?"

"I don't see why I should. Because nearly all the girls there have been to bed with my husband, do you mean? If I were to let that worry me, I shouldn't have a single woman friend left, except those who were past it."

They were interrupted by the arrival of a young woman, a vivacious little doll, who rushed up to the lady of the house, flung her arms around her, and exclaimed:

"My poor darling!"

On the way downstairs, Maigret, pausing to mop his face with a handkerchief, mumbled:

"That's a very strange woman."

A few steps lower down, he added:

"Either I'm much mistaken, or we're nowhere near the end of this case."

To be fair, he reflected, Jeanne Chabut was at least to be commended for her frankness.

# CHAPTER 4

At about five o'clock there was a discreet knock on Maigret's office door. Without waiting for an answer, Joseph, an old man, the oldest of the departmental messengers, came in and handed a printed slip to the Chief Superintendent.

*Name: Jean-Luc Caucasson.*

*Object of Visit: The Chabut case.*

"Where have you put him?"

"In the aquarium."

This was the name jocularly given to one of the waiting rooms, which was walled with glass on three sides, and where there were always one or two people waiting to be seen.

"Leave him to stew for a few minutes, then bring him in."

Maigret blew his nose vigorously, went over to the window, and stood looking out for a little while. Then he opened the cupboard where he always kept a bottle of brandy and poured himself a nip.

He was still a little lightheaded, and he had an uncomfortable feeling of stuffiness, as though he were breathing through cotton wool.

He was standing beside his desk, lighting his pipe, when Joseph announced Monsieur Caucasson.

Caucasson did not appear unduly overawed by the atmosphere of the Quai des Orfèvres. He came forward with hand outstretched.

"Have I the honor of addressing Chief Superintendent Maigret?"

By way of reply, Maigret mumbled, "Please take a seat," retreated behind his desk, and sat down.

"You are a publisher of art books, I believe?"

"That is so. I also have a shop on the Rue Saint-André-des-Arts. Perhaps you know it?"

Maigret did not reply, but subjected his visitor to a thoughtful scrutiny. He was a fine-looking man, tall and spare, with a thick crop of well-brushed gray hair. His suit and overcoat were also gray. He wore a slight, self-satisfied smile, which Maigret took to be his habitual expression. He had the look of a pedigreed animal, an Afghan hound, perhaps.

"Please forgive me for taking up your time like this, especially as it's more in my interest than yours. Oscar Chabut was a friend of mine. . . ."

"I know. I also know that last Wednesday night you attended the world première of a film about the Resistance. The film didn't start until half past nine, leaving you ample time to get from the Rue Fortuny to the Champs-Elysées."

"You mean I'm on your list of suspects?"

"Everyone who knew Chabut is more or less suspect, until I have evidence to the contrary. Do you know Madame Blanche?"

He hesitated, but only for an instant.

"Yes. I've been there once or twice."

"With whom?"

"With Jeanne Chabut. She knew her husband went there regularly, and she wanted to see for herself what sort of place it was."

"Are you Madame Chabut's lover?"

"I was. I have no reason to suppose that I was the only one."

"When was this?"

"The last time we met by arrangement was about six months ago."

"Were you in the habit of going to see her at the Place des Vosges?"

"Yes, when her husband was on one of his trips to the South. Almost once a week, in fact."

"Is this what you came to see me about?"

"No. You asked me a question, and I've answered it to the best of my ability. What I really came about was the letters. I suppose you've found them?"

Maigret, still watching him closely, frowned.

"What letters?"

"Private letters, addressed to Oscar. Naturally, I don't mean his business correspondence. I felt sure he must have kept them somewhere, either in his apartment or at the Quai de Charenton."

"And you feel that you have a claim on these letters?"

"Meg, that's my wife . . . Meg, as I say, is a compulsive letter writer, and she has a habit of saying whatever comes into her head. . . ."

"In other words, you want to get back her letters?"

"She had an affair with Oscar. It lasted quite a long time. I caught them together. He seemed very much put out at the time."

"Was he in love with her?"

"He's never been in love in his life. She was just another scalp to add to his collection."

"Are you jealous?"

"I've got used to it by now."

"Has your wife had other lovers?"

"There's no point in denying it."

"So your wife was Chabut's mistress, and you were Madame Chabut's lover? Is that a fair way of putting it, would you say?"

There was a hint of restrained irony in Maigret's voice, but the art-book publisher apparently failed to notice it.

"Did you write any letters yourself?"

"Three or four."

"To Madame Chabut?"

"No. To Oscar."

"To protest about his relations with Meg?"

"No."

He was coming to the awkward bit now, and had assumed an air of studied negligence.

"You don't know much about the art-publishing business, probably. It caters to a very small public, and production costs are extremely high. It sometimes takes years to recover the capital outlay.

"For that reason, backers are essential."

Maigret, the underlying note of irony much sharper now, asked with apparent artlessness:

"Was Monsieur Chabut one of your backers?"

"He was a very rich man. He was making money hand over fist. It occurred to me that he might be willing to help. . . ."

"So you wrote to him?"

"Yes."

"In spite of the fact that he was your wife's lover?"

"That had nothing to do with it."

"Was this after you had found them together?"

"I don't remember the exact dates, but I think so, yes."

Maigret tilted his chair onto its back legs and pressed down the ash in his pipe with his thumb.

"Were you and Jeanne Chabut already lovers?"

"I knew you wouldn't understand. You still cling to the good old-fashioned middle-class virtues, which simply have no meaning in our world. Wife swapping is nothing to us. It's happening all the time."

"I understand perfectly. What you're trying to say is that you approached Oscar Chabut because he was a rich man, and for no other reason?"

"That's it exactly."

"Just as you would approach an industrialist or a banker with whom you were not personally acquainted?"

"If I found myself in difficulties, yes."

"But in this case you weren't in difficulties, were you?"

"I was considering publication of a major work on certain aspects of Asiatic art."

"Did you say anything in the letters that you have since had reason to regret?"

He was growing more and more uneasy and yet managing, somehow, to keep his dignity.

"Let's say that they could be open to misinterpretation."

"In other words, if they got into the wrong hands, if they were read by anyone who didn't share your own broad-minded outlook, they might seem to suggest blackmail? Is that it?"

"More or less."

"Did you press very hard?"

"I wrote three or four letters."

"All on the same subject, and within a short space of time?"

"I was anxious to get the book under way as soon as possible. I already had the text, by a very distinguished authority on the subject."

"Did he pay up?"

Caucasson shook his head.

"No."

"Were you very disappointed?"

"Yes. I'd expected better of him. I didn't really know him."

"He was a hard man, wasn't he?"

"Hard and contemptuous."

"Did he reply by letter?"

"He didn't even bother. One evening, when we were having cocktails at his apartment with about thirty other people, I pursued it, hoping to get an answer there and then."

"And did you?"

"I did, a very brusque one. At the top of his voice, to make sure that others besides myself should hear him, he said:

"'It may interest you to know that Meg doesn't mean a damn thing to me, and as for your goings on with my wife, I couldn't care less. So I'd be obliged if you'd stop nagging me for money.'"

He had looked rather pale when he came into the room, but now he was flushed, and his long, well-manicured hands shook.

"As you see, I'm being perfectly frank with you. I could have kept my mouth shut, and waited to see how things developed."

"Waited to see whether I would find the letters, you mean?"

"They might be found by anyone."

"Have you seen him since?"

"Twice. It didn't stop him from inviting Meg and me to his parties."

"And you went?" murmured Maigret, in mock admiration. "So you believe in forgiving those who trespass against you?"

"What else could I do? He was a brute, but at the same time you could no more resist him than the forces of nature. There must be others who have been humiliated by him, even among our own friends. He couldn't help himself. He had to feel his own power. He didn't ask to be liked."

"I take it you're asking me to return these letters to you?"

"I'd rather they were destroyed."

"Your wife's as well as yours, I presume?"

"If I know Meg, she will have struck an exaggerated note of passionate eroticism. As to my own letters, as I told you, they're open to misinterpretation."

"I'll see what I can do for you."

"You have found the letters, then?"

Instead of replying, he got up and went to the door, to indicate that the interview was at an end.

"Incidentally, do you happen to own a 6.35 automatic pistol?"

"I keep an automatic in my shop. It's been there, in the same drawer, for years. I don't even know the caliber. I don't much care for firearms."

"Thank you. By the way, did you know about your friend Chabut's regular weekly visits, at about the same time, to the Rue Fortuny?"

"Yes. Jeanne and I would occasionally take advantage of them for our own purposes."

"That will be all for the present. If I need to see you again, I'll get in touch."

At last Caucasson left, bumping against the doorpost as he went. Maigret stood watching him until he reached the head of the stairs, then returned to his desk and asked to be put through to the apartment on the Place des Vosges. This took some time, the line being constantly busy.

"Madame Chabut? Chief Superintendent Maigret speaking. I'm sorry to trouble you again, but I've just had a visitor, and there are one or two questions I want to ask you about him."

"I'd be glad if you'd make it quick—I'm terribly busy. But the funeral arrangements are completed at last, anyway. It's to be tomorrow morning, and it will be strictly private."

"Will there be a religious service?"

"Just a brief memorial service. I haven't let anyone know except a few very close friends, and one or two members of my husband's staff."

"Including Monsieur Louceck?"

"I couldn't very well leave him out."

"What about Monsieur Leprêtre?"

"Him, of course. And Oscar's private secretary too, that gangling kid they call the Grasshopper. I've ordered three cars to drive us straight to the Ivry cemetery."

"Do you happen to know where your husband kept his personal letters?"

There was an appreciable pause.

"Believe it or not, I've never given it a thought! I'm just trying to think. He got very few letters addressed to him here at the apartment. Most of his mail went to the Quai de Charenton. Do you have any particular letters in mind?"

"Letters from friends, men and women."

"If he kept them, they must be in his personal safe."

"Where is that?"

"In the drawing room, behind his portrait."

"Have you got the key?"

"It was one of your staff, I think, who brought back the clothes he was wearing on Wednesday. That was yesterday. There was a bunch of keys in one of the pockets. I noticed a safe key among them, but I thought nothing of it at the time."

"I won't take up any more of your time today, but after the funeral . . ."

"It will be all right if you call me tomorrow afternoon."

"Meanwhile, I must ask you to be sure to destroy nothing, not even the smallest scrap of paper."

Would her curiosity get the better of her? he wondered. If so, she would probably lose no time in opening the safe and reading those precious letters.

Next, he telephoned the Grasshopper.

"How are things at your end?"

"Fine! What did you expect?"

"I've just heard that you've been invited to the funeral."

"Yes, I had a phone call. I wasn't expecting it, I must say. I rather got the impression she didn't like me."

"Tell me, is there, by any chance, a safe anywhere in your building?"

"Yes, on the ground floor, in the accountant's office."

"Who has the key?"

"The accountant, of course, and no doubt Oscar had one too."

"Do you happen to know if he kept any personal papers— letters, for instance—in the safe?"

"I don't think so. As a rule, when he'd read his personal letters he either tore them up into little bits or stuffed them into his pocket."

"I'd be glad if you'd ask the accountant, even so, and let me know what he says. I'll hold on."

He took advantage of the interval to relight his pipe, which had gone out. At the other end of the line, he could hear receding footsteps and the opening and shutting of a door, then, a few minutes later, the door opening again, followed by approaching footsteps.

"Are you still there?"

"Yes."

"It's as I thought. There's nothing in the safe but papers relating to the business, and a certain amount of cash. The accountant isn't even sure that it was the boss who had the spare key. It's more likely to be Monsieur Leprêtre, he thinks."

"Thanks."

"Will you be going to the funeral?"

"I don't think so. For one thing, I haven't been invited."

"A church service is open to everybody."

He put down the receiver. He still had a bit of a headache, but he had recovered somewhat from his earlier gloom. He got up and went next door into the Inspectors' Duty Room. Lapointe was typing up his report. He used only two fingers, but he could type faster than most trained secretaries.

"I've had a visitor," murmured Maigret, "the artbook publisher."

"What did he want?"

"To get back some letters. It's inexcusable of me not to have thought of Oscar Chabut's private correspondence. There are sure to be some very revealing letters. Caucasson's are a case in point. He wrote demanding money. . . ."

"Because the wine merchant was having an affair with his wife?"

"Caucasson caught them in the act. Admittedly, he was having an affair with Jeanne Chabut at the same time. . . . But that's just one example. I have a feeling that, when we get our hands on all the letters he kept, we shall find others."

"Where are they?"

"Seemingly, in a safe behind our friend's portrait in the drawing room of the apartment."

"Has his wife read them?"

"Apparently it didn't occur to her to look in the safe. She came upon the key by accident, in one of the pockets of the suit Chabut was wearing on Wednesday."

"Have you told her about them?"

"Yes, and I'm quite sure she'll have read them before the day is out. The funeral is tomorrow. There's to be a memorial service in the Church of St. Paul. She's invited so few people that only three cars will be needed to take them to the Ivry cemetery."

"Are you going?"

"No."

What would be the use? Whoever he was, the wine merchant's murderer was unlikely to give himself away by making himself conspicuous at a funeral.

"I think you're on the mend, Chief. You're not blowing your nose so often."

"Don't talk too soon. Wait and see how I am tomorrow."

It was half past five.

"There's nothing to keep me here till six. I think I'd be better off at home."

"Good night, Chief."

"Good night, boys."

And Maigret, pipe clenched between his teeth, shoulders hunched, turned and walked out of the room. He was still feeling a little weak at the knees.

He slept heavily. If he had any dreams that night, he had forgotten them by the morning. The wind must have changed during the night and, with it, the weather. It was much less cold. Rain was falling in a steady downpour, and the windows were streaked with it.

"Aren't you going to take your temperature?"

"No, I can tell it's normal."

He was feeling better. He drank his two cups of coffee with relish, and once again Madame Maigret rang for a taxi.

"Don't forget your umbrella."

When he got to his office he glanced quickly through the pile of mail on his desk. This was a long-established habit of his. He liked to see if there were any envelopes addressed in a hand he recognized, a letter from a friend, perhaps, or one containing some information that he was waiting for.

Today there was an envelope addressed in block capitals and marked "Personal" in the top left-hand corner. The word "Personal" was underlined three times.

*Chief Superintendent Maigret*
*Officer in Charge of Criminal Investigations*
*38 Quai des Orfèvres.*

He opened this letter first. It contained two sheets of paper of the kind usually to be found in cafés and brasseries. The letterheads had been cut off. The sheets were covered with very neat handwriting, with regular spacing between the words, suggesting that the writer had an orderly mind and was a stickler for detail.

*I trust that this letter will not be held up in your outer office, and that it will receive your personal attention.*

*I have already spoken to you twice on the telephone, but on each occasion I felt obliged to ring off somewhat abruptly for fear that you would be able to trace the call. Although I am assured that this is impossible with an automatic exchange, I was unwilling to take the risk.*

*I was surprised to find no reference in the newspapers to the personal character of Oscar Chabut. Is it possible that there is not one among all those interviewed by the press who was prepared to speak out and expose him for what he was?*

*Instead, he is described as a man of vision, adventurous and persistent, who fought his way to the top and, by his own efforts, created one of the greatest wine businesses in the country.*

*Surely you must see that this is a disastrous state of affairs! The man was a lousy swine. I have already told you so, and I make no apology for repeating it. He was ready to sacrifice everyone and everything to his overweening ambition and delusions of grandeur. In fact, I do not think it would be going too far to say that, on some subjects at least, he was a madman.*

*For it is hard to believe that a man who was perfectly sane could have behaved as he did. Take his attitude to women, for instance. What he wanted, above all, was to debase and defile them. His desire to possess every woman he met was really a desire to reduce them all to the same level, and thereby assert his own superiority. This was why he was always boasting of his conquests, without any regard for the reputations of the women concerned.*

*And what of the husbands? Is it possible that they were ignorant of what was going on? I do not believe it. They too were under his domination, preferring to remain silent rather than incur his open contempt.*

*He felt the need to reduce everyone else in power and stature, in order to enhance his own. Do you follow me?*

*I sometimes find myself thinking of him in the present tense, as if he were still alive, even now that he has, at long last, got his just deserts. No one will mourn his passing, not even his nearest and dearest, not even his father, who, for years, has refused to see him.*

*There is not a word of all this in the newspapers, so that if, in the course of time, you are able to apprehend the man who shot him and, in so doing, put an end to his crimes, he will be an object of loathing to the whole world.*

*I felt I had to make contact with you. I watched you going into the house on the Place des Vosges with another man, whom I took to be one of your inspectors. I caught sight of you also at the Quai de Charenton where, it may interest you to know, things are not quite what they seem. Everything that man touched is contaminated in one way or another.*

*You are seeking the murderer, are you not? Well, that is your job, and I do not hold it against you. But if there were any justice in the world, you would be seeking him, not to condemn him, but to congratulate him.*

*The man, I repeat, was a rotten, lousy swine, wicked and vicious to the core.*

*I conclude, Chief Superintendent, with my respectful good wishes, and my humble apologies for omitting to append my signature to this communication.*

There was, nevertheless, appended to the letter, an illegible scrawl.

Slowly, sentence by sentence, Maigret reread the letter. He had, in the course of his career, received hundreds of anonymous letters, and he had learned to recognize those that deserved to be taken seriously.

In spite of the intemperate language, the accusations in this particular letter were not without foundation, and the portrait of the wine merchant drawn by its author was a fair likeness of the original.

Was this the work of the murderer himself? Was he one of the many victims of Oscar Chabut's lust for power? If so, was he one of the husbands whose wives Chabut had appropriated and then rejected, as was his wont, or was he one of those who had suffered from his ruthless business methods?

In spite of himself, Maigret found that he was identifying the writer of the letter with the limping man who had waited for him across the road from Police Headquarters, and then hurried off toward the Place Dauphine. He was nothing much to look at, yet, in spite of the fact that his clothes looked as though they had been slept in, he was obviously no tramp. Paris was full of such men, men who fitted in nowhere. Some went inexorably from bad to worse, until they touched rock bottom; others committed suicide.

But a few gritted their teeth and hung on, and eventually surfaced again, especially if someone happened to be standing by to give them a helping hand.

In his heart of hearts, Maigret would have liked to hold out a helping hand to this man. In spite of his pathological hatred of Chabut, which appeared by now to be the sole object of his existence, Maigret did not see him as a madman.

Was it he who had murdered the wine merchant? It was certainly possible. He could picture him waiting in the shadows, his fingers gripping the ice-cold butt of the pistol.

As he had promised himself that he would do, he fired one, two, three, four shots and then made off, limping, toward the Métro.

Where had he gone from there? Where did he live? Perhaps he had made for the bright lights of the Grands Boulevards and gone into a bistro for warmth and a private celebration.

The murder of Chabut was not unpremeditated. The man who had perpetrated it had been planning it for a very long time and, no doubt, deferring it, until some final outrage had at last goaded him into action.

And now his enemy was dead, and quite possibly the murderer was discovering that life had suddenly lost all meaning for him. The victim had once again stolen the limelight. His name was on everybody's lips, he was spoken of with admiration, almost as a man of genius. No one had given a thought to the man who had shot him, nor to his reasons for doing so.

So he had telephoned Maigret. Then he had written to him. And he would write again, driven, though he did not know it, by the need to reveal himself, and bring about his own arrest.

The bell was ringing. It was time for Maigret to go to the Chief Commissioner's office for the daily briefing.

"Anything new on the shooting on the Rue Fortuny?"

"Nothing definite. But I think I'm on the verge of a break-through."

"Does that mean there's a scandal in the offing?"

Maigret frowned. He had not told the Chief Commissioner the details of Chabut's personal life, and there had been no mention of it in the papers. Why, then, should he be worrying at this stage about the possibility of a scandal?

Was it that the Chief Commissioner was personally acquainted with the wine merchant, or that Chabut was well known in the circles in which the Chief Commissioner moved? If so, he must certainly know that Chabut had a great many enemies, all of whom had good reason to wish him dead.

Evasively, he replied:

"I can't put a name to the killer yet."

"Be that as it may, you would be well advised to say as little as possible to the press."

Shortly after this he went through the rest of his mail and dictated a few replies to a typist. His back was aching, and he was still feeling a little below par, but at least his nose had stopped running.

Lapointe came in just before noon.

"I hope you won't hold it against me, Chief, but I just couldn't resist it. I know I'm not supposed to do things on my own, but I just had to go to that funeral. There were about twenty people there in all, and the only representative of the staff was Monsieur Louceck."

"No one else that you recognized?"

"As we came out of the church there was a man standing on the sidewalk opposite, looking at me. I tried to get to him, but by the time I had threaded my way through the traffic he had disappeared."

"You don't say! Here, read this."

He held out the anonymous letter. Every now and then, as he read it, the inspector smiled to himself.

"The same man, wouldn't you say?

"Remember, he saw me on the Place des Vosges, at the Quai de Charenton, and, I'm pretty sure, going in through the door of this building. He must have been expecting to see me again this morning at the funeral."

"And he would have seen us together, and so recognized me."

"I think it would be a good idea to have someone watching the apartments on the Place des Vosges this afternoon. I'll probably be calling on Madame Chabut myself, later. Tell him to ignore me. The important thing is for him to keep his eyes open for anyone loitering near the apartments. So far, our friend has shown himself to be a past master in the art of vanishing."

"Shall I go myself?"

"If you like. You do have the advantage of knowing him by sight."

He went home to lunch, which he ate with relish, and afterward had a nap in his armchair. When he got back to the Quai des Orfèvres he put a call through to Jeanne Chabut's number and asked to speak to her. He was kept waiting some time.

"I'm sorry to bother you so soon after the funeral, but I must admit I'm anxious to have a look at your husband's personal letters as soon as possible. I have a feeling I shall learn a lot from them."

"Do you want to come here this afternoon?"

"If it's at all possible."

"I've got someone coming at five. I can't get out of that, I'm afraid. Could you possibly come right away?"

"I'll be with you in a few minutes."

Lapointe was already watching the apartments. Maigret got Torrence to drive him there and then sent him back to the Quai des Orfèvres. The black draperies, embroidered with silver tears, no longer adorned the front door, and the little sitting room, where the body had lain, was back to normal. Only the scent of chrysanthemums persisted.

She was wearing the same black dress as on the previous day, but she had added a clip of colored stones, which made it look less severe. She was as neat as a new pin, and completely self-assured.

"I suggest we use my sitting room. The drawing room is far too big for just the two of us."

"Have you opened the safe?"

"I must confess I have."

"How did you get it open? Did you know the combination?"

"Of course not. But I realized that my husband probably kept it somewhere on his person, so I went through his wallet. Inside his driving license, I found a slip of paper with a string of figures, so I tried them out on the safe, and they worked."

On top of a Louis XV chest there was a rather bulky parcel, clumsily tied with string.

"I'd better tell you right away that I haven't read all of them. It would have taken all night. I was surprised to find how many he'd kept. I even found my old love letters, written before we were married."

"I think I'd better work backward. I'm more likely to find a clue to the murderer in the later letters."

"Sit down, won't you?"

To his astonishment, she put on a pair of spectacles. They transformed her. He could see now why she wanted to take the business in hand. Here, he realized, was a woman with nerves of steel and a will of iron. Once she made up her mind to a thing, she would never give up.

"These are all short notes. Ah! Here's one signed 'Rita.' I don't know which Rita that would be. . . . It just says: *'I shall be free tomorrow at three. Usual place? Love and kisses, Rita.'*

"Not much given to sentimental outpourings, is she? I must say, I don't care for her stationery. I think scented notepaper is in pretty poor taste, don't you?"

"Is it dated?"

"No, but it was in a bundle with a lot of letters, all of them recent."

"Did you come across any from Jean-Luc Caucasson?"

"So you know about him! Has he been to see you?"

"He's extremely anxious about those letters of his."

It was still raining, and the tall windows were spattered with zigzag streaks. The apartment was very quiet and restful. Between them lay a pile of letters, several hundreds of them, the abstract and brief chronicle of a man's life.

"Here's one. Shall I read it to you?"

"I'd rather read it myself, if you don't mind."

"Do smoke your pipe, if you want to. It won't bother me in the least."

*My dear Oscar,*

*For a long time I could not bring myself to write to you on this subject but, on reflection, we are such old friends that I feel I may venture to do so.*

*It is, as you can imagine, extremely distasteful to me to raise the subject of money, especially knowing what a brilliant businessman you are as compared with myself, who, alas, have no head for figures!*

*Art publishing is a unique business, quite unlike any other. One is always on the lookout for the work that will bring one financial reward as well as critical acclaim. Sometimes one has to wait a long time for it, and when one does eventually discover it one may find oneself without the resources needed to publish it.*

*This is precisely the position in which I now find myself. Business is very sluggish at present—it is more than a year since I brought out my last book—and, as luck would have it, just when things are at their lowest ebb I have the opportunity of publishing a work of exceptional merit entitled 'Certain Aspects of Asiatic Art.' I am confident that this is a great book, and that it will have the success it deserves. In fact, I am virtually certain of being able to sell the rights in the United States for a sum which would cover the production costs many times over.*

*But publication would entail an initial outlay of two hundred thousand francs, of which I cannot produce a centime myself. Admittedly, there is Meg's little nest egg, but that does not amount to more than ten thousand francs or so.*

*Can you see your way to lending me this money? It will seem a trifling sum to you, I know. This is the first time I have ever asked for money in this way, and I confess I find it extremely embarrassing.*

*Before I finally made up my mind to write to you, I consulted Meg, and she said she felt sure that you were too good a friend to both of us to refuse to help.*

*I will be glad to go and see you at home or at either of your offices, whichever suits you best. Just call me or drop me a line to say when and where, and I shall be there. I shall be only too willing to put my signature to whatever written undertakings you may require of me.*

"Sickening, isn't it?"

Seeing that she had just lit a cigarette, Maigret lit his pipe.

"Did you notice the reference to Meg? The second letter is much shorter."

Both letters were handwritten. He had small, neat handwriting, but it was a little shaky here and there.

*My dear friend,*

*I am surprised that you have not yet found time to reply to my letter. It took a lot of courage to write to you in the first place. I would not have opened my heart to you as I did, if I had not had the fullest confidence in you.*

*The situation has deteriorated somewhat since I last wrote. A number of heavy bills will shortly be falling due, and unless I can meet them I may be forced to leave the country.*

*Meg, who knows just how things stand, is very upset. Indeed, it is she who has urged me to write to you again.*

*I trust I shall soon be vindicated in my belief that friendship is not just an empty word to you.*

*I am relying on you, as, I am sure I need not tell you, you can rely on me.*

*Yours . . .*

"I don't know how that strikes you, but it reads like a veiled threat to me."

"Yes," growled Maigret. "It's quite clear."

"Wait till you see what Meg has to say!"

He picked up one of the letters at random.

*My dearest darling,*

*It seems an eternity since I saw you last, though in fact it's barely a week. It was so good to be in your arms and feel the beating of your heart. I feel so safe when I'm with you!*

*I dropped you a note the day before yesterday saying I wanted to see you. I was at the usual place at the time I mentioned, but you never came, and Madame Blanche said you hadn't telephoned.*

*I'm worried. I know how busy you are, and how important your work is, and I realize I'm not the only one. I'm not jealous, and I never will be, so long as you don't drop me altogether. I need you. I long for you to crush me in your arms until it hurts. I long even for the smell of you.*

*Write soon. I don't expect a long letter, just the date and time of our next meeting.*

*Jean-Luc has a lot of worries at the moment. He's got some book or other in mind which, according to him, is going to bring us fame and fortune. How insignificant he is, compared with a real man like you!*

*I long to kiss every part of you.*

*Your very own*
*Meg*

"There are lots more in the same vein, some of them pretty candidly erotic."

"When was the last one written?"

"Before we went on vacation."

"Where did you go?"

"To our place in Cannes. Oscar had to fly back to Paris a couple of times. Some of our friends were there at the same time, but not the Caucassons. I seem to remember they have a little cottage somewhere in Brittany, in one of those villages where all the artists congregate."

"Are there any other begging letters?"

"I haven't nearly finished reading them yet. But there's one, a note from Estelle Japy. She's a widow, an enterprising soul, as you will see. Oscar and she were pretty thick for a time."

*My dear friend,*

*I enclose a bill which, I regret to say, I am unable to meet. I look forward to seeing you in the near future.*

*Yours,*
*Estelle*

"Is the bill enclosed with the letter?"

"I didn't see it. I've no idea what it was for, or for how much. A piece of jewelry, maybe, or a fur coat? She was in church this morning, but she didn't go on to the cemetery."

"Would you mind if I took these letters home with me? Or if you'd rather, I could look in on Sunday, and finish reading them then."

"I hate to refuse you anything, but to tell you the truth I don't want to part with them, even temporarily.

"Come whenever you like, tomorrow if you wish, and I'll leave you alone to read them in peace. There are a couple more I think you should see before you go. There's this one from

Robert Trouard, the architect, asking my husband to put up the capital for the building of some luxury apartments."

"Did he ever invest in any project of that sort?"

"Never, as far as I know."

"What about Trouard's wife?"

"Of course. Just like the others. Only in her case I don't think her husband knew.

"Now this one you must see. There are six sizzling pages of it. The name of the lady in question is Wanda—she's new to me. Not only does she feel it incumbent upon her to describe in the minutest detail exactly what they did at their last meeting, but she goes on, by a dazzling feat of the imagination, to predict just what they will do the next time. I think she must be a Russian or a Pole. I'm sure Oscar must have had his work cut out, getting her out of his hair.

"Here's another interesting one, from Marie-France, Henri Legendre's wife."

She held out a sheet of pale blue writing paper. The ink was of a somewhat darker blue.

*Darling old horror,*

*I ought to hate you, and I will too, if you don't come to me and say you're sorry very soon. I've just heard the most hair-raising tales about you. I won't say who told me, only that it was one of your other conquests. Anyway, you may not even remember her. I don't see how you can remember them all.*

*What really riles me is that you should have spoken of me in the way you did at the top of your voice at a cocktail party, in the hearing of at least half a dozen people. Remember? Someone mentioned my name, and you said: 'It's such a pity she's got sagging breasts.' Well, I always knew you were a low-down skunk.*

*Now I have proof of it, but I somehow don't seem to be able to face life without you.*
*Your move.*

"Of course it's all much more fun if you happen to know the people concerned, the lovely Madame Legendre, for instance. I always see her in my mind's eye, sweeping into a drawing room on her husband's arm, with a perfect cascade of diamonds glittering on her bosom.

"And now I really will have to ask you to go. I'm expecting Gérard any minute. Gérard Aubin, the banker, you know. I need his advice on one or two matters. He's someone I can really trust.

"If you'd care to come back tomorrow afternoon . . ."

"I don't think that will be necessary."

"No, of course, you're entitled to spend Sunday with your family."

It would have surprised her to learn that the Maigrets would probably do nothing more exciting than they usually did on Sundays, which was to spend the afternoon in a local movie theater, and then walk home afterward arm in arm.

Outside, in the square, Maigret spotted Lapointe.

"You were right, Chief, but he was one too many for me. That man is as slippery as an eel. I waited as close to the house as I dared, over there by the railing. The garden in the park was almost deserted, because of the rain, but after I'd been there about half an hour I noticed a man sitting on a bench on the far side. I'm almost sure I recognized him. He was wearing a shabby brown hat, and a raincoat over a dark suit.

"I went into the garden and began to walk toward him, but I hadn't gone ten paces when he got up, made off in the direction of the Rue de Birague, and vanished.

"I broke into a run, much to the astonishment of two old ladies who were sitting chatting under one umbrella. I ran as far as the Rue Saint-Antoine, but there was no sign of our friend. One almost has the feeling that he's trailing you, to reassure himself that you haven't slackened off on the job!"

"He probably knows more about the case than I do. If only we could make him talk! Did you come by car?"

"No, by bus."

"We'll go back by bus, then."

They set off, Maigret with his hands deep in his pockets.

# CHAPTER 5

They did not go to the movies after all, as Maigret had planned. The day started with a torrent of rain that beat down on the almost deserted sidewalks of the Boulevard Richard-Lenoir, and by ten o'clock the wind had risen and was blowing in fitful gusts. There were very few people about, only one or two intrepid, blackclad men and women with umbrellas, hugging the walls of the buildings for shelter, on their way to or from Mass.

It was about ten o'clock, too, when the Chief Superintendent started to get dressed, which was most unusual for him. Up to now he had sat about in his pajamas and dressing gown, doing nothing in particular.

His temperature was up again. It was nothing much, just over 100°, but enough to make him feel rather limp and listless. Madame Maigret naturally took advantage of this to make a bit of a fuss over him, and every time she did some little thing for him he scowled with feigned displeasure.

"What are we having for lunch?"

"Roast beef, with braised celery and mashed potatoes."

The Sunday roast. It reminded him of his childhood, except that in those days he had liked his meat well done. There were several little things that day that brought back memories of his childhood.

Safe and warm together in the apartment, they watched the rain beating down. Just before lunch Maigret murmured a little hesitantly, "I feel like an apéritif, a small glass of sloe gin, I think."

She did not attempt to dissuade him. He went over to the sideboard, where, besides the sloe gin, there was a bottle of raspberry liqueur, both from his sister-in-law in Alsace. The raspberry liqueur won. It was deliciously fragrant, and it needed only a sip for the flavor to linger on the palate for as long as half an hour.

"Won't you have a drop?"

"No. You know very well it puts me to sleep."

Appetizing smells were coming from the kitchen, though his nostrils were less sensitive than usual, on account of his cold. He glanced through one or two weeklies, which he never had time to read except on Sundays.

"It's interesting, you know, in some walks of life the ordinary rules of decent conduct seem to have vanished altogether. . . ."

She did not need to ask what he was referring to. He was still, in spite of everything, in spite of himself, absorbed in the Chabut case, and at intervals throughout the day he reverted to it.

"When you have a hundred or more people, all with more or less sound reasons for wishing a man dead . . ."

He was haunted by the thought of the little man with the limp, who was so skillful at getting lost in a crowd, and who always seemed to be lurking in wait for Maigret, wherever he went. Who was he?

He took his afternoon nap in his armchair. He woke to find his wife busy with some sewing. She never could bear to sit doing nothing.

"I slept longer than I intended."

"It will do you good."

"I hope it turns out not to be the flu after all."

He went to turn on the television. It was showing a Western, and he quite enjoyed watching it. Needless to say, there was a villain, and Maigret could not help thinking that in some respects he was not unlike Chabut. Like Chabut, he was always having to prove his strength to himself and other people, and to this end he bullied and humiliated them.

When the picture was over he murmured, recalling his tête-à-tête with Madame Chabut on the previous day in her little sitting room on the Place des Vosges:

"A strange woman, she is."

"Who will be running the business now?"

"She will."

"What does she know about it?"

"Very little. But she'll soon grasp it, and I'm pretty sure she'll make a success of it. I bet you anything you like that, within a year, Monsieur Louceck will find himself out of a job."

He was in the middle of reading an article on deep-sea exploration when he suddenly had a thought. What was it the Grasshopper had said on the subject of the accountant? That he was a newcomer, who had been there only a matter of months. What had happened to his predecessor? Had he left of his own accord or been sacked?

He must find out right away. Trembling with excitement, he looked up the girl's number in the telephone book. He held on for some time, but there was no reply. No doubt the Grasshopper and her mother were at the movies or were visiting relatives. He tried again at half past seven, but there was still no reply.

"Do you think she knows something?"

"Something she didn't attach any importance to, and that's why she didn't think it worth mentioning. Besides, there's probably nothing to it, but I'm so much at sea at the moment . . ."

In spite of everything, it had been an enjoyable day. They had cold cuts and cheese for dinner, and by ten o'clock they had already gone to bed.

Next morning, instead of going straight to the Quai des Orfèvres, Maigret telephoned Lapointe and asked him to come and pick him up in a car.

"I hope you had a restful day, Chief."

"I hardly moved from my armchair the whole day. As a result, I'm feeling a bit stiff. Quai de Charenton!"

The staff were at their posts, but there was no sense of urgency. In fact, there was almost nothing doing, except at the far end of the yard, where men, their heads covered in sacks to protect them from the rain, were rolling barrels from one place to another.

"While you're waiting, you might as well go and have a chat with the accountant."

He went up the stairs, knocked at the door, and was greeted by the Grasshopper with a broad smile. As usual, she looked as though she found life something of a joke.

"You didn't go to the funeral, after all," he remarked.

"The staff were requested not to do so."

"By whom?"

"Monsieur Louceck. He sent a memo around."

"It struck me yesterday that there was something I'd forgotten to ask you. Am I right in thinking that, when I was asking you about the accountant, you said that he was new to the job?"

"He's only been here since the first of July. It's odd you should mention it now."

"Why?"

"Because I was thinking about it only yesterday at the movies, and I intended to tell you the next time I saw you. It's about the former accountant, Gilbert Pigou. He left the firm in June, toward the end of June, if I remember right, and that's why I didn't think to mention him to you."

Maigret was sitting in Oscar Chabut's revolving chair, opposite the Grasshopper, whose long legs were crossed, so that her mini-skirt had ridden more than halfway up her thighs.

"Did he leave of his own free will?"

"No."

"What sort of man was he?"

"Completely colorless. One scarcely noticed him. You've been into the accounting office downstairs, overlooking the courtyard. We call it the accounting office, though in fact all the real accounting is done at the Avenue de l'Opéra. They never get their hands on any of the big stuff down there."

"Was he married?"

"Yes, I think so. I'm sure he was. I remember, he telephoned one day to say he wouldn't be coming in because his wife was having an emergency operation. Acute appendicitis, I think it was.

"He hardly ever opened his mouth, and he seemed to shrink when anyone looked at him. I think people scared him."

"Was he good at his job?"

"It's all pure routine. It doesn't require any initiative."

"Did he seem particularly interested in you, or in any of the other typists?"

"He was much too timid for anything of that sort. He was brought in fifteen years ago or so, when the business was just beginning to expand. He was rather a pathetic soul, really."

"Why do you say that?"

"I was thinking of his last interview with the boss. I'd have given anything not to have been there. I've never felt more miserable in my life. It was ten o'clock in the morning. Oscar had just arrived, having first stopped at the Avenue de l'Opéra. I can see him still, rubbing his hands and telling me to phone down and ask Pigou to come up.

"He seemed to be full of gleeful anticipation, and it worried me.

"'Sit down, Monsieur Pigou. Move your chair a little to the left, the light's better there. I can't stand talking to someone whose face is just a shadowy blur. How are you?'

"'Very well, thank you.'

"'And your wife?'

"'She's well.'

"'Is she still selling shirts in that shop on the Rue Saint-Honoré? It was the Rue Saint-Honoré, wasn't it?'"

The Grasshopper interrupted herself to remark:

"He had an extraordinary memory for detail. He had total recall about people. He'd never met Madame Pigou, yet he hadn't forgotten that she sold shirts on the Rue Saint-Honoré."

"'My wife no longer goes out to work.'

"'I'm sorry to hear it.'

"The accountant gaped at him, not knowing what to think. Then, as cool as you please, Chabut said:

"'You are dismissed, Monsieur Pigou. After today, you will never again set foot in this building. I have no intention of giving you a reference, so it will probably be quite a while before you find another job.'

"He was thoroughly enjoying his little game of cat-and-mouse. I couldn't bear it.

"Pigou sat on the edge of his chair. He seemed bewildered, not knowing what to do, not knowing where to put his hands. I could feel waves of misery coming from him, so much so that it wouldn't have surprised me if he'd burst into tears.

"'Understand this, Monsieur Pigou, there's no future in being dishonest unless you can manage it with some degree of skill and carry it off with something of an air.'

"The accountant was still wrestling with himself, trying to make up his mind what to do. Then he raised his hand and opened his mouth, as if to speak.

"'Here. Take this, I have a copy. It's a detailed record of the sums of money you have stolen from me in the past three years.'

"'For fifteen years . . .'

"'You've been in my employ. Correct. I wonder why you let all those years go by before you started putting your hand in the till?'

"Pigou was deathly pale, and there were tears rolling down his cheeks. He began scrambling to his feet, but Chabut barked at him:

"'Stay where you are. I can't endure having people stand when I'm talking to them. In three years, as you will see if you look at the statement I have just handed you, you have robbed me of three thousand, eight hundred and forty-five francs. A few francs at a time. To begin with, fifty francs, more or less regularly, once a month. Then seventy-five. And on one occasion a much larger sum: five hundred francs.'

"'That was at Christmas.'

"'What of it?'

"'Ostensibly it was my Christmas bonus.'

"'I don't follow you.'

"'My wife had given up work by then. Her health isn't too good.'

"'Are you saying that you stole money from me on account of your wife?'

"'It's the truth. She never stopped nagging me. She said I had no ambition, and that my employers exploited me and paid me less than I was worth.'

"'You don't say!'

"'She would keep on at me about asking for a raise.'

"'And you didn't have the nerve.'

"'What would have been the use?'

"'You've got something there. Men like you are a dime a dozen. You have no qualifications and no initiative. Why should anyone pay you more?'

"Pigou sat motionless, staring down at the desk in front of him.

"'I told Liliane I'd asked for a raise, and that you'd agreed to an increase of fifty francs a month.'

"'Well,' she said, 'your boss hasn't exactly gone overboard, but it'll do for a start.'"

Once again the Grasshopper interrupted herself.

"I was finding it more and more painful to watch. The clearer it became that the accountant was quite unable to defend himself, the more the boss's eyes sparkled with jubilation.

"'It went up to a hundred francs a month a year ago. And last Christmas, I was supposed to have given you a bonus of five hundred francs. In other words, as far as your wife was concerned, you had made yourself quite indispensable to me. Is that it?'

"'I'm sorry. . . .'

"'Too late, Monsieur Pigou. As far as I'm concerned, you no longer exist. It is not beyond the bounds of possibility that, one day, Monsieur Louceck may decide to help himself to my money. I don't trust him any more than I do anyone else. He may even have done so already, but, if he has, he's at least been clever enough to prevent anyone from finding out. And he certainly isn't the man to indulge in petty pilfering, just to impress his wife. If he ever cheats me, it will be on the grand scale, and in consequence I shall take off my hat to him.

"'You see, Monsieur Pigou, you're nothing but a shabby little nonentity. You always have been and you always will be. A constipated little nonentity. Come over here, if you please.'

"As Chabut rose to his feet, I could scarcely prevent myself from crying out:

"'No!'

"Pigou came forward, his arm half raised to protect his face, but Oscar was too quick for him. He slapped him hard on the cheek.

"'That's for trying to make a fool of me. I could turn you over to the police, but I don't choose to. You will now about-face, and walk out of this room for the last time. Get your things together, Monsieur Pigou, and go. You're fit for nothing but the scrap heap, and, what is worse, you're a fool.'"

The Grasshopper fell silent.

"Did he go?"

"What else could he do? He even forgot to take his fountain pen. It's still in his desk. He never came back for it."

"Was that the last you heard of him?"

"For several months, yes."

"Did his wife never telephone?"

"Not till the end of September or early October. Then she came herself."

"Did she see Chabut?"

"She was waiting for him when he got in. In the meantime she wanted to know whether her husband was still working here.

"'Didn't he tell you he'd left us in June?'

"'No. He still went out every morning at the same time, and came back as usual in the evening. And at the end of the month, as usual, he handed over his salary. We didn't have a summer holiday this year, on account of pressure of work, he said.

"'"I'll make it up to you in the winter. I've always had a yen for winter sports."'"

"'Didn't that surprise you?'

"'Well, you know, I never paid much attention to what he said.'"

"She was much prettier than I'd have expected, with a trim little figure. And she was nicely dressed too.

"'I was hoping you might be able to give me news of my husband. He walked out two months ago, and I haven't set eyes on him since.'

"'Why didn't you come sooner?'

"'I was sure he'd be back, sooner or later. . . .'

"She was taking it all very casually. She had large, rather vacant, dark brown eyes.

"'But now, I've got no money left, so . . .'

"At this point, Chabut came in. He looked her up and down, then turned to me:

"'Who is she?'

"'Madame Pigou,' I said. I had no choice.

"'What does she want?'

"'Her husband has disappeared. She thought he was still working here.'

"'Good God!'

"'For some time after he left, he gave her the equivalent of his salary at the end of each month.'

"He turned and looked her full in the face.

"'Didn't you notice anything wrong? I don't know where your husband got the money, but it can't have been easy. Didn't you know he was a thief, a miserable little thief, who wanted to make you believe he'd had a raise in salary? If he's stopped coming home to you, it must be because he's finally gone under.'

"'What do you mean?'

"'A man can keep himself going somehow for a month or two, but after that, he's bound to go under, with no hope of ever surfacing again.

"'Leave us for a while, will you, Anne-Marie.'

"I knew what that meant. It made me sick. I went down into the courtyard to get a breath of air, and half an hour later I saw her come out. She turned her head away as she went past, but I had time to see that she had lipstick smeared all over her cheek."

Maigret was silent. Slowly and deliberately, he filled his pipe and lit it. Then, in a very low voice, he said:

"My dear, do you mind if I ask you a personal question, though it's no concern of mine, I know."

She looked at him a little uneasily.

"Knowing him as you did, how could you remain on intimate terms with him?"

She tried at first to shrug it off.

"Well, if it hadn't been he it would have been someone else. . . . I had to have someone. . . ."

But then her expression changed. Gravely, she said:

"The man I knew was quite different. With me, he didn't feel the need to bully and show off. On the contrary, he let me see how vulnerable he was. He said once:

"'Maybe it's because you're of no account, just a nice kid, and, besides, I know you'd never take advantage of me.'

"He was terribly afraid of dying. It was almost as though he had a presentiment. . . .

"'So help me, God, sooner or later one of those swine is bound to turn on me. . . .'

"I said: 'Why do you go out of your way to make people hate you?'

"'Because I can't make them love me. On the whole I prefer hatred to indifference.'"

As she told him this, she became quite agitated. In a calmer voice, she concluded:

"Well, there it is. I heard no more of Pigou. I don't know what became of him. It never even occurred to me to mention him to you. It seemed like ancient history, really. It was only yesterday, in the movies, that I suddenly remembered that slap in the face."

A few minutes later Maigret went down the stairs, knocked on the door of the accounting office, and went in. Lapointe was there, talking to a nondescript young man in a dark, ill-fitting suit.

"This is Monsieur Jacques Riolle, Chief."

"We have already met."

"So you have. I'd forgotten."

Riolle, somewhat in awe of the Chief Superintendent, had risen to his feet. His office was the darkest and dingiest in the whole building, and for some obscure reason it smelled even more strongly of wine. There were rows of green files on shelves, reminding Maigret of a country lawyer's office. Between the two windows stood an enormous, old-fashioned safe, which dominated the room. The furniture must have been a job lot, picked up in some auction. There were inkstains everywhere, and the desk, which had probably once been in a schoolroom, was defaced with carved initials.

Riolle, intimidated in the great man's presence, shifted his weight from one foot to the other, and Maigret had the feeling that here was another, younger Gilbert Pigou.

"Are you ready, Lapointe?"

"I was only waiting for you, Chief."

They took their leave of the young man, and went out to the little black car.

As they were getting in, Lapointe said, with a sigh:

"I thought you were never coming. It was heavy going, trying to make conversation with that young man. I've seldom met anyone so dull. It was really depressing.

"Even so, I did get him to talk in the end. He's not a certified accountant, but he goes to night school and expects to complete the course in two years. He's engaged to a girl in his home town. He's from Nevers. He can't marry on his present salary, but he's hoping it won't be too long before he gets a raise, which will enable him to set up house. . . ."

"Is she still in Nevers?"

"Yes. She lives with her parents and works in a haberdasher's. He goes home once a month to see her."

Lapointe was well on his way back to the Quai des Orfèvres before Maigret noticed.

"We won't be going back to the Quai just yet. First, I want you to take me to 57B Rue Froidevaux."

They drove along the Boulevard Saint-Michel, and then turned right toward the Montparnasse cemetery.

"Did young Riolle say if he'd ever met his predecessor?"

"No. He applied for the job in answer to an advertisement. He was interviewed by Chabut himself."

"Determined to make sure for himself that the applicant was a nonentity!"

"What do you mean?"

"With the exception of Louceck, all his employees were ineffectual and submissive. He liked to be surrounded by people he could despise. Come to think of it, he despised all his associates, men and women, at home and at work. I'm convinced that he went to bed with all those women only in order to show that he was master and, to some extent, to defile them."

"Here we are, Chief."

"I think it would be better if you didn't come in with me. I'm going to see Madame Pigou. Two of us together would give the game away and might scare her off. Wait for me in that little bar over there."

He pushed open the door of the lodge.

"Which is Madame Pigou's apartment, please?"

"Fourth floor, on the left."

"Is she at home?"

"She should be. I haven't seen her go out."

There was no elevator, so he had to walk up the four flights of stairs, stopping from time to time to get his breath back. The house was clean and in good repair, and the staircase was less dark than it might have been. There was a radio blaring in one of the first-floor apartments. On the second floor a small boy of four or five was sitting on the top step, playing with a model car.

When he got to the fourth floor, Maigret knocked at the door of the apartment, as there appeared to be no bell. He waited for quite a time, and then knocked again, fervently hoping that he would not have to climb all those stairs again later.

He listened with his ear against the door, but could hear no sound from within. Nevertheless, he knocked yet again, this time so sharply that the door quivered on its hinges, and was at last rewarded by the sound of approaching footsteps, or rather the slither of feet encased in bedroom slippers.

"Who's there?"

"Is Madame Pigou at home?"

"One moment."

He waited for over a minute before the door was finally opened, and a young woman, holding her dressing gown together to prevent it from falling open, stood there looking at him questioningly.

"What are you selling?"

"I'm not a salesman. I would like a word with you, that's all.
I'm Chief Superintendent Maigret of the Criminal Investigation
Department."

She hesitated, then stood aside to let him in.

"Come in. I was resting. I haven't been too well lately."

On her way into the living room, she hastily shut the bedroom
door, but not before Maigret had caught a glimpse of the rum-
pled bed.

"Do sit down," she said, pointing to a chair.

The window looked out onto the cemetery, with its rows of
tall trees. The furniture was of the sort to be found in any of
the big stores on the Boulevard Barbès and usually described in
the catalogues as "provincial."

There was a divan with records strewn all over it and, next
to it, a record player on a pedestal table. Apparently Liliane was
in the habit of reclining on the divan and listening to music. On
the floor was an ashtray, overflowing with cigarette ends.

"Is it about my husband?"

"Yes and no. Do you have any news of him?"

"Still not a word. I called at his place of work, only to discover
that he hadn't set foot there for six months."

"How long ago did he leave you?"

"Two months ago. It was at the end of September, the day
when he should have given me his pay."

She was perched on the arm of a chair, and every now and
then her dressing gown fell open to reveal a candypink slip
underneath. It did not seem to worry her. No doubt she lived
in a dressing gown, except when she went out.

"Have you been married long?"

"Eight years. He just happened one day to come into the
shop where I worked, to buy a tie. He took ages choosing it. He
seemed very much smitten. That evening, when I left work,

he followed me. And the same thing happened the next day and the next. For four or five days he followed me, not having the courage even to speak to me."

"Was he living in this apartment then?"

"No. He had a furnished room in the Latin Quarter. He hadn't known me three weeks before he proposed to me. I wasn't too eager. He was a nice enough boy, but nothing to write home about."

"You weren't in love with him, then?"

She blew out a cloud of cigarette smoke, and looked at him.

"Is there any such thing as love? I'm none too sure, myself."

"Just one question, Madame Pigou. Is your husband slightly lame?"

"Yes. He was knocked over by a car, and broke his kneecap. Ever since, he's had a slight limp in the left leg, especially when he walks fast."

"How long ago was the accident?"

"It was before I knew him."

"How long have you known him?"

"Eight years. An engagement, if you can call it that, which lasted a month, followed by eight years of wedded bliss!"

"Did you go on working after you were married?"

"For three years. But it was an impossible situation. Before I left home in the morning I had to get breakfast, wash up, and clean the apartment. We used to meet for lunch in some restaurant, and in the evening I had to do the marketing, cook dinner, and get through the rest of the household chores. It was no life."

He looked at the narrow divan, littered with phonograph records and magazines, and at the overflowing ashtray. Her favorite resting place, no doubt. Very possibly she had been asleep on the divan when he had disturbed her with his insistent knocking.

Did she have lovers? He was pretty sure she did, partly, no doubt, because she had nothing better to do, and partly as a means of escape.

At present she was looking rather sulky, and this, he suspected, was her habitual expression.

"You suspected nothing until your husband disappeared?"

"No. I don't know whether he got another job, but as far as his comings and goings went, he kept to his normal working hours."

"And at the end of the month, he gave you the usual sum?"

"Yes. I allowed him forty francs a month for cigarettes and fares."

"When he didn't come home, weren't you worried?"

"Not all that much. I'm not the worrying kind. I did telephone his office. Some man answered. I asked to speak to my husband.

"'He's not here,' he said.

"'Do you know when he'll be back?'

"'I can't tell you,' he said. 'I haven't seen him for a long time.'

"And he hung up on me. It was then that I began to be a little worried. I went to the police station to see if they could tell me anything. I thought he might have been involved in an accident."

Clearly, she had not troubled her head very much about it.

"Do you know where he is?" she asked.

"No. That is what I came to ask you. Have you no idea where he might have gone?"

"Not to his father, at any rate. He's lived in the same apartment on the Rue d'Alésia for nearly fifty years. That's where Gilbert was born. In fact, he's spent almost the whole of his life in this district. His mother is dead. His father was a cashier in a branch office of the Crédit Lyonnais. He's retired now."

"Did he get on well with his father?"

"Until we were married. His father couldn't stand me, or so I believe. Gilbert, naturally, stood up for me, so relations have been rather strained in the past few years."

"Have you informed his father of his disappearance?"

"There was no point. They only met once a year, on New Year's Day. We used to pay a formal call together, and were treated to a glass of port and a biscuit. He fusses over that apartment like a real old maid."

"How do you think your husband managed to give you the equivalent of his salary for three months after he left his job?"

"He must have got another job."

"Didn't you have any savings?"

"Only debts! The refrigerator isn't entirely paid for yet, and we had a dishwasher on order for last September, but I managed to cancel that just in time."

"Did he have any personal possessions of value?"

"Of course not! Even the rings he gave me are just cheap things. By the way, you haven't told me yet why you are so interested in him."

"He was dismissed at the end of June, because his employer found out that he had been milking the till—not very skillfully, I'm afraid—for the past three years."

"Was he keeping a mistress?"

"No. He only took very small sums, fifty francs a month to begin with."

"So that's where he got his so-called raise!"

"Exactly. You kept telling him that he ought to tackle Monsieur Chabut, and since he hadn't the courage to do so, and knew besides that it would do no good, he decided to falsify the accounts instead. From fifty francs it crept up to a hundred. And then, last Christmas . . ."

"The five-hundred-franc bonus!"

She shrugged.

"The idiot! A fat lot of good it did him. I hope, for his sake, that he's found another job."

"I doubt it."

"Why?"

"Because I happen to have seen him hanging about in the street at various times of the day, when offices and shops are open."

"What has he done? You must want him for something."

"Oscar Chabut was killed last Wednesday by a man who was lying in wait for him outside a house of assignation on the Rue Fortuny. Did your husband have a gun?"

"A small black automatic, given to him by a friend when he was doing his military service."

"Is it still here?"

She got up and shuffled off into the bedroom. He could hear her opening and shutting drawers.

"I can't find it. He must have taken it with him. As far as I know, he's never used it, and I don't know that he ever had ammunition for it. I've never seen any."

She lit another cigarette and, this time, sat not on the arm but in the chair.

"Do you really think he had it in him to kill his boss?"

"Chabut treated him abominably, and on one occasion slapped his face."

"I know him. At least I've met him. What you say doesn't surprise me. He was a great big brute."

"Didn't he tell you what had happened?"

"No, he just said he was glad to be rid of my husband, and that it was good riddance for me too."

"Did he give you money?"

"Why do you ask that?"

"Because it would be in character. It's not hard to imagine how the interview went."

"You must have a very vivid imagination!"

"No, I just happen to know how he treated women."

"Do you mean he treated them all alike?"

"Yes. Did you arrange to meet again?"

"He took my telephone number."

"But he never called you?"

"No."

"You haven't answered my question. Did he give you money?"

"He handed me a thousand-franc note."

"And how have you managed since?"

"As best I can. I've answered a few advertisements, but so far without success."

Maigret got up. He was aching all over, and his forehead was bathed in perspiration.

"Thank you for your co-operation."

"Look, you say you've seen him several times. Surely, then, you ought to have no difficulty in finding him?"

"Provided I see him again, and he doesn't vanish into thin air, as, up to now, he's always managed to do."

"How was he looking?"

"Exhausted, and as if he hadn't slept in a bed the night before. Has he no friends in Paris?"

"Not that I know of. The only people we ever saw were a school friend of mine, Nadine, and the man she lives with. He's a musician. They sometimes came and spent the evening with us. We'd have a couple of bottles of wine, and Nadine's friend would entertain us on the electric guitar."

Probably she had slept with the musician and, no doubt, others as well.

"Good-by, Madame."

"Good-by, Chief Superintendent. If you have any news, I'd be most grateful if you'd let me know. After all, he is my husband. If he really has killed someone, I'd rather know about it. I assume it constitutes grounds for divorce?"

"I believe so."

He made a note of the address of Pigou's father, who lived on the Rue d'Alésia, and went into the little bar, where he found Lapointe reading the afternoon paper.

"Well, Chief?"

"She's a real little bitch. I've never come across a more unsavory crowd than have turned up in this case! Waiter, a glass of rum!"

"Does she know anything that might be of help to us?"

"No. She's never cared for him at all. She gave up work at the very first opportunity, and, as far as I can see, she lies sprawled on a divan from morning to night, playing phonograph records, reading magazines, and smoking like a chimney. I bet there's nothing she doesn't know about the private lives of the movie stars. She wasn't bothered when her husband disappeared, and when I told her it was possible he had killed a man, her only reaction was to ask me whether that constituted grounds for divorce."

"What do we do next?"

"Take me to the Rue d'Alésia. I want a few words with the father."

"Her father?"

"No, his. He's a retired cashier, used to be with the Crédit Lyonnais. He and his son fell out over the marriage."

The father's apartment was a good deal cozier than the son's, and, to Maigret's great relief, there was an elevator. He rang the bell, and almost at once the door was opened.

"Yes?"

"Monsieur Pigou?"

"I am Monsieur Pigou, what do you want?"

"May I come in?"

"Are you selling encyclopedias? If so, you're the fifth this week."

"I'm Chief Superintendent Maigret of the Criminal Investigation Department."

The apartment smelled of furniture polish, and there wasn't a speck of dust anywhere. Everything was scrupulously neat and tidy.

"Please sit down."

They were in a small sitting room, which looked as if it was scarcely ever used. The curtains were partly drawn, and Pigou went over to open them.

"You're not the bearer of bad news, I hope?"

"As far as I know, there's nothing wrong with your son. I just wanted to ask you when you saw him last."

"That's easy. It was on New Year's Day."

He smiled a little bitterly.

"I was foolish enough to warn him against that girl he was absolutely set on marrying. The minute I saw her, I knew she wouldn't do for him. He got on his high horse, and called me a selfish old man, and a good deal more besides. Before that, he always came to see me once a week, but after his marriage he stopped coming, and I only saw him once a year. He called on me with his wife every year on New Year's Day, a very formal visit. He came out of a sense of duty, I suppose."

"Did you bear him any resentment?"

"No. He's completely under her thumb. It's not his fault."

"Has he ever asked you for money?"

"You obviously don't know him. He's much too proud."

"Not even in the last few months?"

"What's happened to him?"

"He lost his job in June, and for three months after that he went out in the morning and came back at night, just as though he were still working at the Quai de Charenton. What's more, at the end of each month, he gave his wife the equivalent of his earnings."

"He must have found another job."

"That's not so easy for a man of forty-five with no qualifications."

"Maybe. All the same . . ."

"He must have got the money somewhere. At the end of September he disappeared."

"You mean his wife hasn't seen him since then?"

"That's right. And someone, not yet identified, shot his former employer, Oscar Chabut, in the street. He put four bullets into him."

"And you think . . . ?"

"I don't know, Monsieur Pigou. That's what I'm trying to find out. I came to see you in the hope that you might be able to help me."

"I know less than you do. His wife didn't even go to the bother of letting me know. Do you think he's done something to be ashamed of, and that's why he's gone into hiding?"

"It's possible. I've seen a man two or three times in the last few days whom I believe to be your son. I have also had two anonymous telephone calls, and a letter written in block capitals which I have every reason to think came from him."

"You didn't tell him . . . ?"

"Tell him what? If he's the man who shot his former employer, then he's playing with fire, almost as if he wanted to get himself arrested. It's more common than you'd think. He has no home and no money. He knows he's bound to be caught sooner or later. He's not ashamed of what he's done. On the contrary, he's more likely to be congratulating himself. Chabut was a despicable character."

"I don't understand."

"I'll keep you informed, Monsieur Pigou. Meanwhile, if you hear anything, I'd be grateful if you'd give me a ring."

"As I said, it's most unlikely that he'll come to me."

"Thank you for your help."

"Was he any help?" Lapointe asked.

"Even less than the wife. He didn't even know his son had disappeared. He's a neat little man, very likable. He spends all his time polishing the floors and the furniture, and he keeps the apartment as neat as a pin. He doesn't have a television set or a radio, at least I saw no signs of them.

"Back to the Quai, now. It's time we got to the bottom of this business."

Within the hour, Maigret and five of his inspectors were assembled in his office for a final briefing.

# CHAPTER 6

**S**it down, all of you. Needless to say, you're welcome to smoke if you want to."

Maigret himself proceeded to light up and, puffing at his pipe, he looked thoughtfully at each of them in turn.

"You all know the main facts. Ever since I started making inquiries into the death of Oscar Chabut, as a result of shots fired when he was leaving a house on the Rue Fortuny, a man has been keeping a close watch on my movements. He's no fool, and he has more than once anticipated my next move. What's more, he's a remarkably slippery customer. I've been close to him once or twice, but he's always managed to slip away and melt into the crowd."

It was already dusk, but it had not yet occurred to anyone to switch on the lights, so that the whole room was in shadow. With so many people in the office—two extra chairs had had to be brought in from next door—it was stiflingly hot.

"I have no evidence that this man is the murderer, only a strong feeling, reinforced by his persistently behaving as if he were guilty.

"This afternoon I discovered his identity and learned something of his history. At first sight it seems almost beyond belief.

"The man in question was an employee of the wine merchant, ostensibly an accountant, but in fact just an underpaid book-keeper, a nonentity. He has been married eight years. His wife, who was a shopgirl when he met her, gave up her job as soon as she decently could, and never stopped reproaching him for not bringing home more money. Make a note of her name and address, Loutrie, I'll explain why later. Liliane Pigou, 57B Rue Froidevaux. It's opposite the Montparnasse cemetery. She spends most of the day half naked, lying on a divan, listening to phonograph records, smoking like a chimney, and reading magazines and comic strips.

"I've called you together this evening, because I feel that the time has come to bring him in, whatever the cost. The likelihood is that he's got a gun, but I don't think he'll attempt to use it.

"I want you, Janvier, to pick six men to patrol the Quai des Orfèvres in relays of two for twenty-four hours. As well as telephoning me twice and writing me a longish letter, the man has been keeping a watch on me here from across the street. I caught sight of him once, but unfortunately he slipped away before I could catch up with him."

The bluish twilight was beginning to deepen. Maigret switched on his green-shaded desk lamp, but not the overhead light, thus illuminating the faces of the men, while leaving the rest of the room in shadow.

"Here's his description. Take it down, all of you: Below average height, say about five foot five. Plumpish though not fat, and very full in the face. He wears a dark brown suit and a crumpled raincoat. He smokes cigarettes. Finally, he has a slight limp. His kneecap was injured in an accident some years ago, and as a result his left foot turns over a little as he walks."

"Dark hair?" asked Loutrie.

"Brown hair and eyes, yes, and rather thick lips. Although he's shabby and obviously at the end of his tether, you wouldn't mistake him for a tramp.

"The reason I want two men on duty all the time is that he's so remarkably good at vanishing.

"Is that clear, Janvier?"

"Yes, Chief."

Maigret turned to fat Loutrie, who was smoking his pipe in little puffs.

"What I've just said to Janvier applies to you too. I'm not asking any of you to go on watch yourselves, just to make sure that your men are in position, and that they are relieved at regular intervals."

"I'll see to that."

"Now you, Torrence. You'll need a team of six, like the others. The stakes are high. I can't risk letting him slip through our fingers again. Your men are to cover the Chabuts' place on the Place des Vosges. Madame Chabut is a beautiful woman of about forty. She's extremely elegant and gets her clothes from the top fashion houses. She has a Mercedes and a chauffeur. It's just possible that she may decide to go out in her husband's car, so you'd better also be looking out for a red Jaguar convertible."

They exchanged glances, like a class of schoolchildren.

"And you, Lucas. You're to cover the Quai de Charenton. Today being Saturday, the offices and warehouses will probably be deserted this afternoon, and tomorrow too. There may be watchmen or caretakers on duty. I don't know."

"I see, Chief."

"I think that covers all the places where he's most likely to turn up. Usually he keeps watch from a little way off. He seems to be obsessed with finding out what we're up to. Sometimes he's close on our heels, and at others he's one jump ahead.

"I can't help wondering whether he hasn't a kind of unconscious longing to get caught."

"What about me?" asked Lapointe.

"I want you here on call, ready to come and get me and drive me anywhere, at any time of the day or night. It will also be your job to take any messages that may come in, and keep me informed by telephone."

Under the impression that he had finished, they half rose from their chairs, but Maigret motioned them to remain seated.

"There's one very puzzling thing. This man lost his job at the end of June. It appears that he had no savings, at least not to his wife's knowledge, and remember, he was in the habit of handing over his pay envelope to her every month. He got no salary for June, because his employer refused to pay him, on the grounds that he had a right to retain the money in part compensation for the thefts. Nevertheless, on June 30th the man went home and handed his wife the equivalent of a month's salary.

"From then until the end of September, he continued to leave home at the usual time every morning, and to return at the usual time in the evening. All this time, of course, his wife had no idea that he was no longer working at the Quai de Charenton.

"I presume he tried to get another job, but failed to do so.

"In September he vanished. It was then, I think, that he decided to give up the struggle, and, from what I've seen of him, he hasn't slept many nights in a bed since then.

"But he had to have some money, if only a few francs to buy food. Now, if there's one place that seems to have an irresistible fascination for down-and-outs, it's Les Halles. I wonder where they'll all go in a few months' time, when the market is transferred to Rungis."

The telephone rang.

"Hello! Chief Superintendent Maigret? It's that man again. The one who always asks to speak to you personally."

"Put him through."

Looking up, he said to his men:

"It's him! Hello! Yes, I'm listening. . . ."

"You've been to see my wife. I thought you would. You were with her a long time, and your assistant waited for you in a bar nearby. Is she terribly angry with me?"

"Not in the least, as far as I could tell."

"Is she very unhappy?"

"That isn't how she struck me."

"Did she say anything about money?"

"No."

"I can't think how she manages."

"She went to see Chabut some weeks ago, and he gave her a thousand francs."

The man at the other end sniggered.

"What did my father say?"

It was staggering. He was aware of Maigret's every move. Yet he had no car, and was certainly in no position to take taxis. Apparently he had managed to limp all over Paris without being seen, and when anyone did catch sight of him he vanished as if by magic.

"He didn't say very much. I gather he doesn't terribly care for your wife."

"What you mean to say is that he detests her. It was on account of her that we quarreled. I had to choose between him and her. . . ."

In Maigret's opinion, he had backed the wrong horse.

"Why not come and see me here, at the Quai des Orfèvres, for a chat? If you didn't kill Chabut, you'll be free to come and go as you please. If you did kill him, then I can recommend a good lawyer, who will at least make a plea for clemency, even if he doesn't manage to get you acquitted. Hello! Hello! . . ."

Gilbert Pigou had rung off.

"You heard that? He already knows I've been to his apartment to see his wife, and that afterward I called on his father."

It was a kind of game, and up to now Pigou had won all along the line. And yet he wasn't particularly bright. Quite the contrary, in fact.

"Where was I? Oh, yes. Les Halles. In the whole of Paris, it's the one place where a man on the run is most likely to end up. By tonight, I want twelve men going through the whole area with a fine-tooth comb. They can get help if they need it from our colleagues in the Ist Arrondissement, who know the district inside out."

Of course, it was always possible that all this elaborate planning would lead to nothing. But there was no harm in hoping, though it now seemed unlikely that Pigou would fall an easy victim to Maigret's schemes. As likely as not, he was at this very moment looking up at the lights in Maigret's office windows from across the street.

"Well, boys, that's it."

They all got up, like schoolboys, and were making for the door when Maigret spoke again.

"One very important point. I don't want any of your men carrying guns. And the same goes for you. Whatever happens, whatever the cost, I don't want him shot at."

"What if he shoots first?" grumbled fat Loutrie.

"I said 'whatever the cost.' But, he won't shoot. I want him brought in sound in wind and limb."

It was half past five. Maigret had done all he could. Now he could only wait. He was tired, and he had still not quite recovered from his bout of flu.

"Hang on a minute, Lapointe. What do you think of my strategy?"

"It might work."

Clearly, the Inspector was none too hopeful.

"If you want my honest opinion, either he'll fall into our clutches by sheer accident—and that may not be for days or weeks—or he'll go on eluding us until he decides to give himself up."

"I'm inclined to agree with you, but I had to take some steps. I'll be glad if you'll drive me home. I'm longing to get into my slippers and sit by the fire. Or rather, to tell you the truth, I'm longing to get to bed."

He was very flushed, and his throat was sore. Perhaps this was not flu at all, but quinsy?

As they drove out of the forecourt, Maigret looked about him with interest, but there was no sign of the shabby figure of the man who was so much on his mind.

"Stop at the Brasserie Dauphine."

He had a nasty taste in his mouth and a sudden craving for a glass of very cold beer. It couldn't wait till he got home.

"What will you have?"

"Same as you, a beer. It was very stuffy in your office."

Thirstily, Maigret gulped down two glasses of beer, then wiped his mouth and lit his pipe. The Châtelet was ablaze with Christmas decorations and lights strung across the street. From one of the big stores, loudspeakers were broadcasting seasonal music.

When they reached the Boulevard Richard-Lenoir, Maigret once more looked searchingly up and down the street, in the hope of seeing Pigou, but there was no one about who even remotely resembled him.

"Good night."

"I hope you're feeling better tomorrow, Chief."

He took the stairs slowly, but nevertheless he was out of breath when he reached the top. Madame Maigret was waiting for him on the landing. She could see at a glance that he was no better, and that it was beginning to get him down.

"Hurry up and come in out of the cold."

He was not cold. On the contrary, he was much too hot; he was drenched with perspiration. He took off his heavy overcoat and his muffler, loosened his tie, and, with a sigh, slumped into his armchair.

"I've got the beginnings of a sore throat."

She was not unduly worried; an attack of flu, lasting a week or two, was more or less an annual occurrence with him. He was inclined to forget this, and could never quite shake off his dread of being permanently handicapped by illness.

"Any phone calls?"

"Should there have been?"

"I was half expecting one. He called me up at the Quai just now, and he must know my home address. He's extremely restless at the moment, and feels under some sort of compulsion to keep in touch with me."

This was not the first case of its kind that he had come across. Years ago there had been a murderer who had written him a letter several pages long, every day for a month. Each had been written in a different brasserie, but in that instance the man had not cut off the letterheads. The only hope of catching him would have been to put a watch on every brasserie and café in Paris, and there were not enough men available.

One morning, on his way to his office, Maigret had noticed an elderly little man sitting patiently in the glass-walled waiting room generally referred to as the aquarium.

It was the man he had been looking for.

"What's for dinner?"

"*Raie au beurre noire.* I hope it's not too rich for you."

"There's nothing wrong with my stomach."

"What about asking Pardon to look in on you?"

"Leave the poor man alone. He's got enough to do, caring for people who are really ill."

"Would you like your dinner in bed?"

"What! And have the sheets soaked through in an hour?"

He did, however, agree to get undressed. Comfortable in pajamas, dressing gown, and slippers, he settled down with the newspaper, but his mind was not on it. His thoughts kept returning to Pigou, keeper-of-the-petty-cash turned thief, on account of his wife, who had taunted him with being frightened of his boss. And he had been frightened of him, far too frightened to ask for a raise.

Where was he at this moment? Did he have any money left at all? If so, how and where had he got it?

Then there was Chabut, arrogant, irresistibly impelled to shower contempt on others and make himself universally detested. In business he had been insolently triumphant, yet he had remained as vulnerable as in the days when he had tramped from door to door in the hope of securing an order for a case of wine.

He was not the first man, in Maigret's experience, whom insecurity had driven to mete out punishment to all those within his orbit.

"Dinner is ready."

He was not hungry. Nevertheless, he ate what was put before him. He had some difficulty in swallowing his food. Tomorrow he would probably have lost his voice.

By now, the men from the Quai des Orfèvres would all be at the posts assigned them by Maigret. At the last minute, he had been tempted to add:

"And you'd better set a watch on my apartment on the Boulevard Richard-Lenoir as well."

But some obscure feeling, of decency perhaps, had deterred him.

It was almost as though he were afraid of something. He got up from the table and went across to the window. It was not raining, but a strong east wind was blowing, which meant that colder weather was on the way. He saw a pair of lovers go by, arm in arm, stopping every few yards to kiss.

Two policemen on motorcycles, wearing capes, went past the window, presumably on routine patrol. There were lights in most of the windows across the street, and behind the net curtains shadowy figures could be seen, in one case, an entire family sitting at a round table.

"Do you want to look at television?"

"No."

There was nothing he really wanted to do except grumble, as was his wont when he was not feeling well, or when a case had dragged on too long.

He was determined not to go to bed before his usual time, and he settled down once more to try to read the paper. But half an hour later he was back at the window, peering into the street, in the hope of catching sight of a figure which was beginning to seem familiar to him.

The boulevard was deserted, except for a passing taxi.

"Do you think he'll come here?"

"How should I know?"

"Are you expecting new developments?"

"There's always a possibility. I may get a phone call from Lapointe."

"Is he on duty?"

"He'll be on all night, to take any messages that may come in."

"Do you think your man is beginning to crack?"

"No. He hasn't lost his nerve yet. He doesn't seem to realize the predicament he's in. All his life, he's been the underdog. He's never known what it means to hold his head high. And now, all of a sudden, he feels, in an odd sort of way, free. The entire police force is looking for him, and he has managed to elude us all. That's quite a feather in his cap, you see. For the first time in his life he's important, he matters."

"And he'll feel even more important, when he stands trial."

"That's just it, and he can't make up his mind whether to give himself up or to keep on going with his little game of cat-and-mouse."

He returned to his newspaper. His pipe was alight and, although he was not enjoying it, he went on smoking as a matter of principle. He too was unwilling to surrender. He was not going to allow the flu to get the better of him. His eyelids were inflamed and his eyes smarting, but he was determined to keep them open.

At half past nine he got up from his chair and returned to the window. On the pavement opposite stood a man gazing upward, apparently at the windows of the apartment.

Madame Maigret, sitting at the dining table, looked up to speak, but was silenced by what she saw. Her husband's broad back was turned toward her. He was tense and motionless, and looked, somehow, larger than life.

There was something mysterious, almost awe-inspiring, in his sudden stillness.

Maigret watched the man, scarcely daring to breathe, lest he frighten him off, and the man looked back at him, although he could probably see nothing but a bulky shadow behind the muslin curtains.

Once, at Meung-sur-Loire, while he was lounging in a deck chair, Maigret had seen a squirrel come down from the plane tree at the bottom of the garden.

For a time, the squirrel had remained motionless under the tree, and Maigret had seen the rise and fall of its silky breast fur in time to the beating of its heart. Then, with extreme caution, it had inched forward, and stopped again.

Maigret had watched it, scarcely daring to breathe, and the little russet creature had stared back at the man as though fascinated, yet with every muscle taut, ready for instant flight.

It had been like a slow-motion film interspersed with stills. The squirrel, growing bolder, had reduced the distance between them by a yard or more. For a further ten minutes, it had continued to advance cautiously, until there was barely a yard between it and Maigret's hand hanging over the side of the chair.

Had the squirrel wanted to be stroked? Not then, at any rate. Its bright glance traveled from the hand to the face, then back again, and in a couple of bounds it was back in the tree.

Maigret recalled the incident as he stood gazing fixedly at the shadowy figure of the man across the street. Gilbert Pigou, like the squirrel, seemed fascinated by the Chief Superintendent, whom he had, in a sense, been stalking for days.

But, like the squirrel, he was tense and ready to take flight at the slightest alarm. The Chief Superintendent knew that it would be useless for him to dress and go downstairs. By the time he got outside, there would be no one in sight. It would be equally useless to alert the nearest police station.

Was he trying to pluck up the courage to cross the street and come into the house? That was not impossible. He had no friends, no one whom he could trust.

He had made up his mind to act, and he had done so. He had killed Oscar Chabut. Afterward, he had fled. Why? An instinctive reaction, no doubt. What would he do next? Keep on the run?

As with the squirrel, it went on for all of ten minutes. At last the man took a step forward but, immediately regretting it, or so it seemed, turned on his heel and, with one last backward glance at Maigret's window, made off in the direction of the Rue du Chemin-Vert.

The bulky frame of the Chief Superintendent relaxed. He remained for a moment at the window, as though to recover himself, then went across to the sideboard to get his pipe.

"Was it her?"

"Yes."

"Did he mean to come and see you, do you think?"

"He was tempted. I think he's afraid I'll be a disappointment. Men of his sort are terribly sensitive. They long to talk, to make themselves understood, and yet they don't really believe there is anybody capable of understanding them."

"What will he do now?"

"Walk, most likely, but God knows where to. He'll walk on and on, alone with his thoughts, and muttering aloud to himself."

He scarcely had time to sit down in his chair when the telephone rang. He picked up the receiver.

"Yes?"

"Chief Superintendent Maigret?"

"That's right."

He recognized Lapointe's voice.

"We're getting results already, Chief, thanks to the efforts of our colleagues in the Ist Arrondissement, in particular Inspector Leboeuf, who knows Les Halles like the back of his hand. Until about two weeks ago Pigou had a room, if you could call it that, on the Rue de la Grande-Truanderie."

Maigret knew the street. There, at night, one had the illusion that the days of the Beggars' Opera had returned. It swarmed with the dregs of humanity, in search of some stinking bistro, where they could get a bowl of soup or a glass of red wine. Many spent the night there, dozing in a chair or propped up against a wall. There were almost as many women as men, and they were by no means the least drunken and filthy.

It really was a human sewer, fouler even than the darkest places under the bridges. In the old, cobbled roadway, outside the roominghouses, lingered still more women, most of them aging and hideous, waiting for the men to come out.

"He was staying at the Hôtel du Cygne. Three francs a day for an iron bed with a straw mattress. No running water. Toilets in the back yard."

"I know it."

"Apparently he spent most of the night unloading fruit and vegetables from the trucks. He didn't get in till morning, and he slept half the day."

"When did he leave the hotel?"

"The owner says he hasn't seen him for two weeks. Needless to say, he lost no time in renting the room to someone else."

"Are they still searching the district?"

"Yes. There are about fifteen men on the job. The inspectors in the Ist Arrondissement can't think why we haven't had a full-scale raid, such as they carry out from time to time."

"That's the last thing we want! I hope you told them not to do anything rash."

"Yes, Chief."

"No news from the others?"

"Not a word."

"Pigou was here, on the Boulevard Richard-Lenoir, just a few minutes ago."

"You mean you saw him?"

"From my window. He was on the sidewalk, just across the street."

"Didn't you go out to him?"

"No."

"Is he still there?"

"No, but he may come back. If so, he'll probably hang about for a while trying to make up his mind, and then, quite possibly, make off again."

"Have you any more instructions for me?"

"No. Good night."

"Good night, Chief."

Maigret's head was aching. Before going back to his armchair, he poured himself a small glass of sloe gin.

"Won't it make you perspire?"

"Well, you always say grog is the best cure for flu. Incidentally, though, Pardon doesn't agree with you."

"It's time we had them to dinner. We haven't seen them for over a month."

"Let me get through with this business first. Lapointe had some news. We now know where Pigou was living until recently. It's a crummy joint in Les Halles, with the charmingly poetic name of Hôtel du Cygne. He may have been there for months."

"Has he left it?"

"Yes, two weeks ago."

Maigret was determined not to go to bed before what he considered to be a reasonable hour, and, according to him, that meant not before ten.

He made still another attempt to read the paper, but he kept darting surreptitious glances at the clock. He did manage to take in the first few lines on the front page, but after that the words no longer made any sense to him.

"You're dead tired."

"We'll go to bed in ten minutes."

"You'd better take your temperature."

"If you say so."

She went to get the thermometer. Obediently, he put it in his mouth, and kept it there for five minutes.

"A hundred and one degrees."

"If you've still got a temperature tomorrow, I'm sending for Pardon, whether you like it or not."

"Tomorrow's Sunday."

"Sunday or not, Pardon won't mind."

Madame Maigret went into the bedroom to undress. She went on talking to him with the door open.

"Your throat is raw. I don't like it at all. I'm going to paint it in a minute."

"You know it makes me sick."

"You won't feel a thing. You said you were going to be sick last time, and you weren't."

She returned armed with a bottle of viscous liquid, the main ingredient of which was methylene blue, and a little brush. It was an old-fashioned remedy, but Madame Maigret still believed in it, after more than twenty years.

"Open wide."

He could not resist taking one last look out of the window, before closing the shutters and going to bed.

There was no one standing on the sidewalk across the way. The wind was blowing harder and harder and raising the dust all the way down the central section of the boulevard.

He fell into a deep, feverish sleep from which it took him a long time to return to the surface. He felt the touch of living flesh on his arm, insistently. His first reaction was to recoil from it.

It was a human hand, and it seemed to be trying to communicate some sort of message to him. Once more he pushed it away and turned over on his side.

"Maigret . . ."

It was his wife's voice, but so soft as to be barely audible.

"He's out there on the landing. So far, he hasn't plucked up the courage to ring the bell, but he's tapped on the door once or twice, very gently. Can you hear me?"

"What's that?"

He stretched out his hand, switched on the bedside lamp, and looked about him in bewilderment. He had been dreaming. He had already forgotten his dream, but he still had the feeling of having come back from a long way off, from another world.

"What did you say?"

"He's here. He keeps tapping on the door, very gently."

He got out of bed and put on his dressing gown, which was lying on a chair.

"What time is it?"

"Half past two."

His pipe lay half full on the bedside table. He relit it.

"You don't think there's any danger he might . . . ?"

He switched on the living-room light on his way to the front door, and stood absolutely still for a moment before opening it.

The light on the stairs, which was operated by a time switch, had long since gone out, and the man stepped out of darkness into the patch of light streaming from the doorway. He seemed at a loss for words. No doubt he had a speech prepared, but, on seeing Maigret within arm's length of him, wearing a dressing gown and with his hair all disheveled, he was so overwhelmed that he could do no more than stammer:

"I'm disturbing you, am I not?"

"Come in, Pigou."

It was still not too late for him to bolt down the stairs and escape, for he was a good deal younger and more agile than the Chief Superintendent. Once he had crossed the threshold it would be too late, and Maigret, as he had done with the squirrel, was careful to remain absolutely still.

Probably the man hesitated for no more than a few seconds, but it seemed much longer. Then he took a step forward. For a moment, Maigret considered locking the door and pocketing the key, but finally, with a little shrug, he decided against it.

"You must be cold."

"It's not exactly warm outside. There's a biting wind."

"Here, sit down. You'd better keep your raincoat on until you've warmed up a bit."

He went to the bedroom, where his wife was getting dressed, and called through the door:

"Make us a couple of grogs, will you?"

Then, feeling as though a great weight had been taken off his shoulders, he sat down opposite his visitor. It was the first time he had seen him at close quarters. Seldom, if ever, had he been so eager to learn more about anyone than about this man.

What surprised him most was that Pigou looked so young. His round, rather chubby face was immature, almost child-like.

"How old are you?"

"Forty-four."

"You don't look it."

"Did you order the grog especially for me?"

"For me too. I've got flu, and possibly quinsy as well. It will do me good."

"I don't drink as a rule, except for a glass of wine with my meals. I daresay you've noticed how dirty I am. I haven't been able to keep my things clean for a very long time, and it's a whole week since I washed in hot water—that was at the public baths on the Rue Saint-Martin."

As they talked, they were keeping a close watch on one another.

"I've been expecting you for quite a while."

"You saw me, then?"

"Not only that, but I could sense your uncertainty. You took a step forward, and then turned on your heel and made off toward the Rue du Chemin-Vert."

"I saw you at the window, but I wasn't sure whether you could see me, since I wasn't standing under a lamp."

At the sound of approaching footsteps he started, just as the squirrel would have done. It was Madame Maigret with their drinks. Considerately, she avoided looking at him.

"Do you want some sugar?"

"Yes, please."

"Lemon?"

Having added the sugar and lemon, she put the glass down on the table in front of him. Then she served her husband.

"If you need anything, just call."

Later they might want more grog. Who could tell?

It was obvious that Pigou had been well brought up and that correct behavior was important to him. Holding his glass in his hand, he waited for the Chief Superintendent to drink before taking a sip himself.

"It's scalding hot, but it does one good, don't you think?"

"At any rate, it will warm you up. Now perhaps you'd like to take off your coat."

He did so. His suit, which was quite well cut, was very wrinkled and badly spotted. There was a long streak of white paint on the jacket.

Suddenly they were tongue-tied. Both knew that when they spoke again it would be to discuss matters of grave import, and, for quite different reasons, neither was eager to begin.

The silence continued for a long time, as they both sipped their grogs. Then Maigret got up to refill his pipe.

"Do you smoke?"

"I'm out of cigarettes."

There was a pack in the sideboard drawer. Maigret offered it to his visitor. Pigou looked uneasily at Maigret, and could scarcely believe his eyes when his host lit a match and held it out to him.

When they were once more seated opposite one another, Pigou said:

"I must, first of all, apologize for bursting in on you like this, and in the middle of the night, too. . . . I didn't have the courage to go to the Quai des Orfèvres. And I just couldn't go on alone, walking all over Paris forever."

There was not so much as a flicker of his eyes that Maigret was not acutely aware of. Here, in the intimacy of his own home, with a glass of grog in his hand, he looked like a benign uncle, to whom one could safely confide one's most intimate secrets.

# CHAPTER 7

**W**hat's your opinion of me?"
These were almost the first words he had spoken, and it was clear that it was a question of crucial significance to him. No doubt he had spent the greater part of his life searching people's faces to find out what they thought of him.

What could one say?

"I don't know very much about you yet," murmured Maigret, with a smile.

"You're very kind. Do you always treat criminals so considerately?"

"I can be very rough at times."

"With whom?"

"Men like Oscar Chabut, for instance."

Suddenly, Pigou's eyes lit up. At last he had found a friend.

"I admit I stole a little money, but it was nothing to him, hardly as much as he would hand out in tips in a month. But if anyone was a thief, he was. He robbed me of my manhood, my self-respect. He degraded me to the point where I was almost ashamed to be alive."

"What finally induced you to put your hand in the till?"

"I'd better tell you everything, I suppose."

"Why else should you have come here?"

"You've seen my wife. What did you make of her?"

"I know very little about her.

"I think perhaps she looked on marriage as a way out of having to earn a living. What surprises me is that she went on working for three years."

"Two and a half years."

"What she most wanted was to queen it in a cozy little home of her own. Some women are like that."

"You realized that, did you?"

"It was pretty obvious."

"I often had to do the housework myself, when I got home in the evening. If she'd had her way, we would have eaten out every night, to spare her the trouble of cooking a meal. I don't think she can help it. It's something about her metabolism. Her sisters are the same."

"Do they live in Paris?"

"One is in Algiers. She's married to an engineer, who works for a petroleum company. The other lives in Marseilles and has three children."

"Why didn't you have children?"

"I wanted to, but Liliane wouldn't hear of it."

"I see."

"She has another sister, and a brother who . . ."

With a shake of the head, he pulled himself up.

"But there's no point in going on about them. Don't think I want to blame anyone but myself. . . ."

He took a gulp of rum and lit another cigarette.

"I'm keeping you up, and it's so late. . . ."

"Go on. Chabut humiliated you, and so did your wife."

"How did you know?"

"She was always complaining that you didn't earn enough to live on, wasn't she?"

"She kept saying she couldn't think why she married me.

"And then she would sigh and say:

"'Am I to live my whole life in two rooms, and even without a cleaning woman?'"

He was looking not at Maigret but at a patch of carpet. It was almost as though he were talking to himself.

"Was she unfaithful to you?"

"Yes, before we had been married a year. I didn't find out until two or three years later. One day I left the office early to go to the dentist, and I saw her with a man, near the Madeleine. She was clinging to his arm, and then I saw them go into a hotel together."

"Did you say anything to her?"

"Yes, but according to her it was all my fault. I couldn't give her the kind of life a girl has a right to expect. In the evenings I was always half asleep, and it was all she could do to drag me out to a movie, that sort of thing. And besides, I was no good in bed. . . ."

He flushed as he spoke. This last insult must have wounded him more keenly than any other.

"Three years ago—it was on her birthday—I took some money from the petty cash. It was just enough to pay for a decent dinner, and I took her to a restaurant on one of the Grands Boulevards.

"I told her I was expecting a raise very soon.

"'It's about time,' she said. 'Your boss should be ashamed of himself, paying you such a miserable pittance. If I ever see him, I'll tell him a thing or two.'"

"You only took small sums?"

"Yes. To begin with I told her I'd had a raise of fifty francs a month. It wasn't long before she was complaining that that wasn't enough, so I raised it, so to speak, to a hundred francs."

"Weren't you afraid of being found out?"

"It had almost become a habit. No one ever checked my books. And besides, considering the enormous turnover of the business, it all amounted to so very little."

"One time you took a five-hundred-franc note."

"That was at Christmastime. I pretended I'd had a bonus. I almost came to believe it myself. It made me feel less of a worm, somehow.

"I've never had a very high opinion of myself, you see. My father wanted me to follow in his footsteps and take a job with the Crédit Lyonnais, but I couldn't face the thought of competing with people much more capable than I was. I was happy in my little office at the Quai de Charenton, where I was virtually my own master."

"How did Chabut find out?"

"He didn't. It was Monsieur Louceck. Once in a while he would look in to see what I was up to. This time he must have noticed something amiss, but he didn't say a word to me. You'd think he'd have asked for an explanation, wouldn't you? But no, he behaved as though nothing was wrong, and went straight off and told Monsieur Chabut."

"That was in June, wasn't it?"

"Yes, the end of June, the twenty-eighth, to be exact. Shall I ever forget it! He sent word that he wanted to see me in his office. His secretary was there, but he didn't send her out of the room. I didn't mind, because, to tell you the truth, it never entered my head that I'd been found out."

"He told you to sit down."

"Yes. How did you know?"

"The Grasshopper, Anne-Marie, I mean, told me the whole story. After the first few minutes, she felt as uncomfortable as you did."

"It made it worse for me, being trampled on like that in front of a woman. He said the most humiliating and wounding things. Looking back, I'd much rather he'd handed me over to the police.

"I honestly believe he enjoyed every minute of it. Each time I thought he'd finished, he came back with something worse. Do you know, he even taunted me because I took so little?

"He claimed he would have had some respect for a real thief, but not for a petty pilferer like me."

He stopped for a moment to get his breath back. He had been speaking with some vehemence, and his face had become scarlet. He took another sip of rum. Maigret did so too.

"When he said, 'Come here!' I hadn't the least idea of what he intended to do, but I was frightened anyway. He slapped me full in the face with tremendous force, I could feel the imprint of his hand for quite a while after.

"No one had ever raised a finger to me before. Even when I was a kid my parents never smacked me. I just stood there swaying, stunned. He said something like:

"'Now get out.'"

"I can't remember whether it was then or earlier that he told me he wouldn't give me a reference, and that he'd see to it that no reputable firm would give me a job."

"He felt humiliated as well," murmured Maigret, very gently.

Pigou's head jerked up, and he gaped at Maigret in astonishment.

"Didn't he actually say that no one could make a fool of him with impunity?"

"You're right, he did. It never occurred to me that that was what was at the back of everything he did. Do you think he was really mortified?"

"More than that. He was a strong man, or thought he was, and he had succeeded in everything he had ever undertaken. Don't forget that he started as a door-to-door salesman.

"As far as he was concerned, you hardly existed. You were little more than part of the furnishings of an office on the ground floor, where he practically never set foot. He probably thought that it was an act of charity to keep you on at all."

"That would be like him, yes."

"He was in need of reassurance, just as you were, and that's why he wanted to possess every woman who came his way."

Gilbert Pigou raised his eyebrows. Suddenly he felt uneasy.

"Are you saying that he was to be pitied?"

"All of us are to be pitied, to a greater or lesser extent. I'm just trying to see things as they are. It's not my business to apportion blame. You left the Quai de Charenton. Where did you go from there?"

"It was eleven o'clock in the morning. I'd never been out at that time. It was a very hot day. I walked past the Bercy warehouses, in the shade of the plane trees, and then went into a bistro somewhere near the Pont d'Austerlitz. I had two or three brandies, I think. I don't remember very clearly."

"Did you have lunch with your wife?"

"She'd stopped meeting me for lunch long before that. I walked for miles, and drank a great deal, and then, because my shirt was sticking to me, I went into a movie theater to cool down. Do you remember last June? It was a scorcher."

Clearly, he was anxious to tell the whole story, in the minutest detail. He desperately needed to get it off his chest. Maigret was a sympathetic listener. He was attentive to every word, and obviously interested. Pigou felt he owed it to him to leave nothing out.

"When you got home in the evening, didn't your wife notice you'd been drinking?"

"I told her that my colleagues had treated me to an apéritif to celebrate my promotion and transfer to the Avenue de l'Opéra."

Far from smiling at his naïveté, Maigret looked very grave.

"How did you manage, two days later, to give your wife the equivalent of a month's salary?"

"I had nothing saved up. She allowed me just forty francs a month for cigarettes and fares. I had to find some sort of job. I lay awake all night thinking about it. When I left in the morning, I told her I wouldn't be home to dinner, because I'd have to spend most of the evening getting things straight in my new office.

"I had forgotten, the previous day, to hand in the key of the safe before leaving. I knew there would be an unusually large sum of money in the safe, as the next day was payday.

"From time to time over the years, I'd had to go back to the office at night to finish some urgent job or other. On those occasions I would take the front-door key home with me.

"Once I forgot it. I walked around the building, trying to find a way in, then I remembered that the back door, which had warped, didn't close properly, and could be prized open with a penknife."

"Wasn't there a night watchman?"

"No. I waited till it was dark and crept into the courtyard. The little door opened, as I had hoped it would. I went into what used to be my office, opened the safe, and grabbed a bundle of notes. I didn't even wait to count them."

"Was it a large sum?"

"More than I earned in three months. That evening I hid the money on top of the wardrobe, keeping back just the equivalent of a month's salary. I left home at the usual time. I just couldn't bring myself to tell Liliane that I'd got the sack."

"Why did it matter to you so much what she thought of you?"

"Because there was no one else. For years, she, and she alone, had witnessed my life and actions. She was critical, of course, but in a way I think she trusted me.

"I went out every day to look for another job. I thought, at first, it would be easy. I read the small ads and applied in person for whatever there was. Sometimes there were queues of people waiting, nearly all of them old and hopeless. I felt really sorry for them.

"I was asked questions, starting with my age. Usually, when I told them I was forty-four, that was the end of it.

"'Thirty is the upper age limit. This is a job for a young man.'

"I thought of myself as a young man. I felt young. As the days went by, I became more and more discouraged. After a couple of weeks I realized I couldn't be choosy. By then I'd have been quite contented to be an office boy or a shop assistant.

"At best, they took my name and address, and said, 'You'll be hearing from us.'

"Those who thought I might be suitable asked me about my last job. Naturally, in view of Chabut's threats, I dared not tell them.

"I said, 'I've done a bit of everything. I've been abroad a good deal.'

"As I don't speak anything but French, I had to pretend I'd worked in Belgium and Switzerland.

"Then they asked for my references. I said I'd send them.

"Needless to say, those people never heard from me again.

"The end of July was even worse. Many offices were closed down, or the bosses were away on vacation. I took home my salary as usual, or rather I got the necessary amount from my supply on top of the wardrobe.

"'You haven't been yourself lately,' my wife said. 'Is the work more tiring in your new office?'"

"'It's just that it takes a little time to get used to. I'm having to learn to work with computers. All the sales side of the business is dealt with at the Avenue de l'Opéra, and there are more than fifteen thousand retail outlets. It's a great responsibility.'

"'When do you get your vacation?'

"'I won't be able to manage a vacation this summer. Maybe at Christmastime. I've always thought a winter holiday in the snow would be fun. You could go away, though. Why not go home to your family for three or four weeks?'"

Did he himself recognize the pathos, indeed the tragedy, of what he was saying?

"She went away for a month. She spent two weeks with her parents in Aix-en-Provence, where her father is an architect, then she went on for another couple of weeks to stay with one of her sisters, the one with three children, who had rented a house at Bandol for the summer.

"I felt utterly lost all by myself in Paris. I went on going to the Rue Réaumur to see what jobs were available, and applying for any I thought might do, but with no more success than before.

"I was beginning to realize that Chabut had been right. I would never get another job of any kind.

"I began to haunt the Place des Vosges, where he lived, not with anything especially in mind but just in the hope of seeing him, but he, like so many others, was away on holiday, probably in Cannes, where they have an apartment."

"Did you hate him?"

"Yes. With my whole being. It seemed so cruelly unjust that he should be basking in the sun while I was looking for work, almost alone, it seemed to me, in Paris.

"There was enough money left on top of the wardrobe for me to give my wife the equivalent of another month's salary and still have a little for myself.

"And after that? What was there left to do but confess the truth to my wife? I was certain she'd leave me. She's not the sort who would stay with a man who was no longer able to support her."

"Did you still care for her?"

"I think so. I don't know."

"And now?"

"She's become a stranger to me. It happened gradually, I think, but now I can't imagine why what she thought or didn't think should have mattered so much to me."

"When did you see her for the last time?"

"She got back from the South at the end of August. I gave her my so-called salary. I stayed on another three weeks with her, although I knew that this time I wouldn't be able to give her anything at the end of the month.

"I decided one morning to go and not come back. I took nothing with me except the few hundred francs that were left."

"Did you go straight to the Rue de la Grande-Truanderie?"

"So you know about that? No. I took a room in a cheap but respectable hotel near the Bastille, where there was no risk of running into my wife."

"Was that when you started following Oscar Chabut?"

"I knew where he was likely to be at most times of the day, so I hung around the Quai de Charenton, the Avenue de l'Opéra, and the Place des Vosges. I also knew that almost every Wednesday he went with his secretary to the Rue Fortuny."

"What did you have in mind?"

"Nothing. He was the man who had ruined my life, robbed me of my self-respect, and deprived me of all hope."

"Were you armed?"

Pigou put his hand in his trouser pocket and drew out a small, bluish, automatic pistol. He got up and laid it on the table in front of Maigret.

"I took it with me in case I should decide to kill myself."

"Were you ever tempted to do so?"

"Often, especially at night, but I was too scared. I've always been afraid of violence, of physical pain. Chabut may have been right. Perhaps I am a coward."

"I must interrupt you for a moment to make a telephone call. You'll see why, shortly."

He dialed the number of the Quai des Orfèvres.

"Put me through to Inspector Lapointe, please, Mademoiselle."

Pigou opened his mouth as if to speak, but he said nothing.

Madame Maigret was busy in the kitchen preparing fresh grog.

# CHAPTER 8

Is that you?" asked Maigret.

"Why aren't you in bed, Chief? You don't sound as if you've just waked up. There's no further news."

"I know."

"How can you know? Where are you speaking from?"

"From home."

"It's three o'clock in the morning."

"You can call off the search. Everyone can go home."

"Have you found him?"

"He's here, opposite me. We've been having a quiet talk."

"Did he come of his own free will?"

"Can you see me running after him down the length of the Boulevard Richard-Lenoir?"

"How does he seem?"

"Fine."

"Will you be wanting me?"

"Not immediately. But don't leave the office. Call in the patrols and let Janvier, Lucas, Torrence, and Loutrie know. I'll call you back later."

He hung up and waited in silence while Madame Maigret took away the empty glasses and handed them full ones.

"I forgot to say, Pigou, that although we are together like this, here in my apartment and not at the Quai des Orfèvres, I am still a police officer, and I reserve the right to make what use I think fit of anything you may tell me."

"I understand."

"Do you know a good lawyer?"

"I don't know any lawyers, good or bad."

"You'll need one tomorrow, when you appear before the Examining Magistrate. I'll give you some names."

"Thank you."

Following the telephone call there was a slight chill in the air. Both men felt a sense of strain.

"Your very good health."

"The same to you."

And, making a jest of it, he added:

"I daresay it will be a long time before I see another glass of grog. I'm in for a very stiff sentence, am I not?"

"What makes you think that?"

"First of all, because he was a man of wealth and influence. And secondly, because I've no excuse to offer."

"When did you first get the idea of killing him?"

"I don't know. First I had to give up my room near the Bastille, and that's when I moved to the Rue de la Grande-Truanderie. Things were very tough after that. I spent most of the night unloading vegetables in Les Halles, and I didn't get to bed until the early hours of the morning. I used to cry myself to sleep. The smell was nauseating. Even the noises were sickening. I felt as if I had been exiled from the civilized world to a kind of limbo, unlike anything I had ever known before.

"I still spent my days lurking in the vicinity of the Place des Vosges, the Quai de Charenton, and the Place de l'Opéra. Once or twice I even spied on Liliane, hiding in the shadow of the trees in the Montparnasse cemetery.

"More and more often, whenever I caught sight of Chabut, I found that I was muttering to myself:

"'I'll kill him!'

"It was no more than an empty threat. I had no real intention of killing him. I was standing on the side lines, so to speak, watching him live his life. I observed his big red car, his self-satisfied face, his beautifully cut, freshly pressed clothes.

"In contrast, I was going rapidly downhill. I had left the Rue Froidevaux taking only the suit I was wearing. By now it was terribly creased and covered with spots. My raincoat was far too thin to keep out the cold, but I couldn't afford to buy an overcoat, not even a secondhand one.

"As it happens, I was watching the Quai de Charenton offices from a distance when Liliane went there. Presumably, she had gone first to the Avenue de l'Opéra, as I'd told her I had been transferred there.

"She was in there a long time. At one point, I saw Anne-Marie come out into the yard for a breath of air, and I guessed what had happened.

"I wasn't jealous. It was just one more slap in the face. The way that man behaved, you'd have thought he owned the earth. Once more, I found myself muttering:

"'I'll kill him!'

"I moved off, dragging my foot. The last thing I wanted was to be seen by my wife."

"When did you first go to the Rue Fortuny?"

"About the end of November. By that time I couldn't even afford a Métro ticket."

He gave a bitter little laugh.

"It's an odd sensation, you know, not having any money in one's pocket, and knowing that never again will one be able to live like a normal human being. Most of the people one meets in Les Halles are old, but there are a few young ones, and they all have the same lost look. I have it too, haven't I?"

"No."

"I should have, because there's no difference now between them and me. What I brooded over most was that slap in the face. He ought not to have hit me. I might have got over the things he said, wounding and humiliating though they were. But he slapped me as he would a naughty child."

"Last Wednesday when you went to the Rue Fortuny, did you know that it was to be for the last time?"

"I wouldn't have come here if I hadn't made up my mind to tell you everything. I didn't know I was going to kill him. That's the truth, I swear it. Believe me, I wouldn't lie to you, of all people."

"What was your state of mind?"

"I felt I was reaching the end of my tether. I couldn't sink any lower. Sooner or later I was bound to be picked up in a police raid, if I wasn't carried off to the hospital first, suffering from exhaustion and starvation. Something was bound to happen soon."

"What, for instance?"

"I thought of paying him back in kind. I imagined him coming out of that house with Anne-Marie. I would go up to him and raise my hand. . . ."

He shook his head.

"But, of course, it was out of the question, really. He was so much stronger than I was. I waited there till nine o'clock. I saw the light go on in the hall. He came out alone. The gun was in my pocket, but it didn't take a second to whip it out.

"I didn't really take aim. I just fired again and again, three or four times, I think, I can't remember now."

"Four."

"I had no thought of running away, at first. I meant to stay there and wait for the police. But then I began to think what they might do to me. I was afraid of being knocked about. So I started running toward the Métro on the Avenue de Villiers. No one followed me. Almost before I knew it, I was back in Les Halles, and signing on as a vegetable porter. I couldn't face a whole night alone in that room.

"Well, there you are, Chief Superintendent, that's the whole story."

"What prompted you to telephone me?"

"I don't know. I felt so isolated. I didn't think anyone would ever understand. I'd often read pieces about you in the paper. I'd always wanted to meet you, and by that time I'd almost made up my mind to put a bullet through my head.

"I longed to talk to someone just once, before I died. But I was frightened the whole time, not of you, but of your men."

"My inspectors don't knock people about."

"I've heard it said that they do."

"People say all sorts of things, Pigou. Have a cigarette. You're not still frightened, are you?"

"No. I telephoned you a second time and then, almost immediately afterward, I wrote you a letter from a café on the Boulevard du Palais. I felt very close to you. I would have liked to follow you about the streets, but you were always in a car. I had the same problem with Chabut.

"So I had to try to put myself in your place, guess where you were likely to go next, and get there before you.

"That's how I came to be waiting for you when you went to the Quai de Charenton. I was certain that Anne-Marie would tell you about me. In fact, I can't imagine why she didn't that very first day.

"But then, the scene with Chabut took place in June, and I suppose it seemed like ancient history to her.

"I saw you on the Place des Vosges too."

"And at the Quai des Orfèvres."

"Yes. I didn't see any point in keeping out of sight, because by then it seemed inevitable that I should be caught. It wouldn't have been long before I was arrested, would it?"

"If you had stayed in Les Halles, you would almost certainly have been found and arrested tonight. By ten o'clock, it was known that you had had a room in the Hôtel du Cygne. From there, it was just a matter of searching all the neighboring bistros to find you. Had you taken to drinking?"

"No."

Most men, in similar circumstances, would have drowned their sorrows in drink.

"I intended originally to go to the Quai des Orfèvres, and ask to be taken to you. But then I thought they'd probably turn me over to just any inspector who happened to be on duty, and I probably shouldn't be allowed near you. So I came to the Boulevard Richard-Lenoir."

"I saw you."

"I saw you too. I meant to come up to your apartment. You were standing there in your dressing gown, framed in the window with the light behind you. You looked enormous. All of a sudden I took fright and made off as fast as I could. I wandered about the district for hours. I came back at least five times, but by then the lights were out in your apartment."

"Excuse me a minute."

He dialed the number of the Quai des Orfèvres.

"Put me through to Lapointe, please. Hello! Have you sent all the men home? Is there anyone there with you?"

"Lucas is on night duty, and Janvier has just got in."

"I want you and Janvier here as soon as possible with a car."

"Will they take me away?" Pigou asked, when Maigret had replaced the receiver.

"I'm afraid so."

"I understand. All the same, I'm nervous. It's like going to the dentist."

He had killed a man. He had come to Maigret of his own free will. Even so, it was fear that was uppermost in his mind. Fear of being beaten up and ill-treated.

He had almost forgotten that he was a murderer.

Maigret was reminded of the boy, Stiernet, who had done his grandmother to death by hitting her repeatedly with a poker, and who had as good as said:

"I didn't mean to do it."

He subjected Pigou to a long, hard stare, as though trying to see into his innermost being. The accountant looked back at him uneasily.

"Is there anything else you want to ask me?" he said.

"I don't think so. No."

What was the use of asking him if he was sorry for what he had done on the Rue Fortuny? Was Stiernet sorry for what he had done?

No doubt, the question would be put to him at the Assizes, and if he answered it truthfully there would be a murmur of disapproval in the courtroom.

There was a long silence, while Maigret drank the remains of his grog. Then they heard a car draw up, followed by the opening and shutting of a door.

He refilled and lit his pipe, more to keep himself in countenance than because he felt like smoking. Footsteps sounded on the stairs. He went to open the door. The two inspectors peered into the living room with frank curiosity. A cloud of bluish smoke drifted across the ceiling light.

"This is Gilbert Pigou. We have had a long talk. Tomorrow we will proceed to the official interrogation."

The accountant looked at the two inspectors. Their appearance reassured him a little. They did not look the sort of men who would beat anyone up.

"Take him to the Quai and see that he gets a few hours' sleep. I'll be in myself around midday."

Lapointe made a sign to him. He was so tired and bemused that he did not, at first, understand it. Once more Lapointe pointed to the handcuffs, as if to say:

"Shall I put them on?"

Maigret turned to Pigou.

"It's not that we don't trust you," he murmured, "but we have to comply with the regulations. They will be removed as soon as you get to the Quai des Orfèvres."

On the landing, Pigou stopped and took one last look at Maigret. The very sight of the Chief Superintendent seemed to give him courage. There were tears in his eyes.

But were they not simply tears of self-pity?

*Epalinges*
*September 29, 1969*